A
LOVER'S
HATE

RAMSEY TESANO SAGA
II

ALTONYA WASHINGTON

A LOVER'S HATE

For my awesome and supportive readers, your patience has been truly inspiring. I do hope this will be worth the wait.

FIRST PROLOGUE

Phoenix, Arizona~ 1 year earlier…

Something was…not right and Jesus was that putting it all in the mildest of terms. Despite their weird- *another mild term-* relationship over the last…How long had it been?

Smoak Tesano leaned forward in the cushioned pine-framed chair as if weariness prevented him from exhibiting more perfect posture. Bracing elbows to knees, he fought to clear his mind of some of its clutter.

Simply put, he knew her. He knew her too well to believe that what had just happened was simply part of her having a *rough* day. There was more and what unsettled him most was that he didn't believe she had the slightest clue of how to explain it. He'd wait for her to awaken. *That* would tell the tale or at least a portion of it.

Then what? The last thing he wanted to do was to scare her. God knows he'd had enough of doing that.

A Lover's Hate

She'd come to Phoenix for their annual meeting. He refused to go to Las Vegas which left her little choice but to accommodate him and make the trip to the research compound/home he kept on the outskirts of the Sonora Desert. As he'd given her free reign to develop the land in Vegas, she couldn't very well argue with him about making the trip to sign the papers to renew their agreement.

Well…she could have argued…The wide set of; what could only be described as an artfully sculpted mouth, curved into a knowing smile. He'd had enough knock down drag outs with Sabra Mariette Ramsey to know no word or deed ever passed between them without upset.

Smoak admitted that he was to blame for it. He'd accepted that long ago and figured since he was on such a roll, why stop? They didn't really have to see each other in person every year to renew the agreement originally crafted by his grandfather, her uncle and her father back when he and Sabra were in college.

The fucking land was little more than a payoff anyway, he thought, smoothing the back of his hand across a jaw as perfectly set as the rest of the face it was attached to. At least the land had been a payoff in *his* opinion. Liam Tesano was on the express train to the afterlife and wanted to clear his conscious.

Smoak recalled the way his parents urged him to take the olive branch. He did it for their sakes… and to maintain ties with Sabra. Seeing her every year that way was only an additional weight to the punishment- the guilt he piled on his shoulders since the day he'd turned his hate on her.

Movement from the bed caught his eye and ear and Smoak tilted his head a fraction. Soft, barely vocal moans surged from past Sabra's parted lips. Smoak was focused on the sounds she made. Her moves captured a great deal of his focus as well. He couldn't look away from her hips rotating beneath the sheets as they tangled around her long, maple brown limbs.

She appeared to be waking from the depths of a dream. A wet one, Smoak thought if the sounds of her then heightened moans were any clue. Working harder to keep his focus then, he smoothed both hands across his head taking time to faintly rub his fingers into the sleek hair that he refused to let grow into a full mass of waves. The close cut cap covered his scalp in an abundance of jet black.

He muttered a curse which mingled with the sounds of her moans. He'd have to wake her else wind up in bed with her…again. He'd pulled the heavy armchair to the foot of the bed where he'd watched her sleep for the last four hours. Leaning close, he squeezed her foot before she'd moved it out of his reach amidst her writhing.

"Sabra? Sabe?" he squeezed her other foot and repeated the move just once more before she jerked awake and upright in a puddle of hunter green coverings.

Smoak couldn't see her face clearly enough but he knew she had to sense him there before her in the chair. He wasn't an easy thing to see in pitch black so he gave her a few moments to make an attempt to get her bearings.

"Smoak?" her voice was as faint as her moans had been.

"Mmm hmm," he gestured after allowing just a couple of additional silent moments. He next flipped on a lamp in the corner from where he'd gotten the chair.

Light illuminated the small bedroom in the bungalow of the inn where she usually stayed during the contract renewal meetings. Awkwardly, Sabra covered herself as best she could with the wrinkled sheets that were haphazard on the bed. Eventually, her toffee colored stare drifted up to his face.

Smoak's uncertainty merged into understanding. "God…" he murmured mere seconds before the bell buzzed near the front of the bungalow.

Sabra; desperate to leave the room, scooted from the bed with the top sheet trailing behind her as she went to see to the door.

Greeting a guest was last on her list and she continually checked over her shoulder expecting to see Smoak following her out into the small living room. She pulled open the door and received something of a shock when she turned to find the bell ringer leaning half in half out the door.

The first thing that occurred to Sabra was how tall the woman was. That was saying a lot considering she was close to 6'1 herself. The woman before her had to be close to 6'3. Sabra's intrigue over the woman's height eased off quickly as she then grew preoccupied by the strange, child-like grin that seemed so out of place on someone so… imposing.

Sabra realized she was gawking and most likely frowning then. She was most definitely not a morning person. Between Smoak Tesano in her bedroom and this bitch in her doorway, Sabra accepted the fact that her day wasn't shaping up to be one of the all-time greats.

"Yes?" Sabra hoped her tone came across as snappy and no-nonsense. No-nonsense in spite of the fact that she was standing in the door wearing nothing but a sheet.

Whatever the tone, it didn't seem to faze the woman leaning on the doorjamb. Her hand; appropriately sized given her height as well as her rather muscular build, rested flat on the door. In and of itself, the stance relayed a silent message for Sabra to reconsider any thoughts of slamming the door shut. Not one to scare easily, she couldn't deny feeling the distinct chill of unease when she glared into the woman's disturbingly blank green eyes. The vibrant color contrasted against the woman's deep brown skin and made her gaze appear even more peculiar.

"Sabra Ramsey."

It wasn't a question. The woman leaned in a bit further beyond the threshold. Sabra had to step back lest they'd be rubbing noses.

"Who wants to know?" Sabra decided she'd had enough of the early morning weirdo and her tone of voice then left no confusion as to how pissed she was. Still, a tiny fissure of uncertainty appeared in the stone intensity of her glare then.

The woman had pushed off the jamb to her full height. *Yep, 6'3 easy*, Sabra thought and swallowed around a lump of unexpected...fear? She didn't think she'd ever been happier to hear Smoak's voice.

"Sabe?"

The rich depth of his bone-melting octave sent relief filtering into her toffee stare. Sabra didn't dare look away from the woman, who was then ramrod straight and as alert as a big cat ready to pounce. Earlier, Sabra had rushed from the bedroom to escape Smoak. Just then she was taking refuge in his presence. The woman's penetrating eyes held a look that screamed- unstable!

Smoak took a fistful of the sheet that made a sarong about Sabra's body and pulled her none too gently behind him.

"Help you?" he inquired of the woman, looking down at her from his considerable height advantage.

A Lover's Hate

The green eyed visitor's gaze harbored something crazed- feral in its wildness. The woman tried and failed to straighten her stature enough to gain a few more inches on Smoak. Realizing how useless that course of action was, she curved her hand; which was resting on the door, into a fist and pounded it once. Then, she flashed a quick wicked wink toward Sabra and was gone.

Smoak left the door open to follow the woman's departure and noted that her gait resembled that of a child skipping carefree down a candy-lined path. The comparison was so ludicrous it made him want to laugh in spite of his bewilderment.

Sabra wasn't so amused. Her hand weakened slightly on the sheet. She tripped over the folds of it in a blind trek toward the mini bar next to the credenza. Smoak slammed the bungalow door just as she was reaching for a tiny beaded bottle of gin.

"You can follow the idiot's lead and get out." She said.

"Sabra."

She maintained her grip on the bottle but let it hit the counter space with a pitiful clatter. "Smoak please. I can't not after…*that*." She turned and waved a hand in the general direction of the door.

"I want to talk to you about last night." He approached her barefoot in his stalking stride. The delivery of his words was as slow as his steps.

She shook her head like a stubborn child, sending thick strands of her waist-length mane into her face. "You've already said everything you need to. I'm done being turned down by you." He *had* turned her down, hadn't he? She was in a sheet and he…God…She squeezed her thighs together. The simple act of looking upon his taut blackberry skin; that showed not one imperfection, already had her throbbing on the cusp of something orgasmic.

Where was his shirt? Why couldn't she remember? Oh God, had it happened again? She recalled the gin bottle in hand and let it fall to the carpeted floor with a thud.

"Go." She steeled herself to speak the lone word.

"Talk to me," he countered softly, sweetly and almost pleading.

Again, the childlike shaking of her head ensued. *Ignore it. Ignore it and it goes away.*

"Smoak-"

"No."

"Go."

"Forget it." He wasn't about to leave her after that scene straight from the *Twilight Zone* a few minutes ago.

Sabra tilted back her head as though she were desperate to stifle the tears threatening to shimmer past her sparkling stare.

"Go get cleaned up," he ordered as she was opening her mouth for what appeared to be further protests. "Pack your stuff and I'll take you to the airport." He added, giving her his back until she'd gone to do as he'd said.

When Sabra left the room without further argument, he expelled a breath, braced his fists to the back of the sofa and worked to reign in his guilt, his remorse and his hate.

SECOND PROLOGUE

Phoenix, Arizona~ 6 months ago...

"Recalculating..."

"Piece of crap," Austin Chappell took the GPS from its mount and shook the device as if that would change its behavior. He tossed it across the dash when the guide's computer generated voice wafted out that it was 'recalculating' again.

Austin beat a fist to the steering wheel of the rental he'd set out in that morning. He'd been paying more attention to the rear view mirror since he'd spotted the gray Lincoln Continental there twenty minutes prior.

The car had dipped in and out of view all the while he'd been in the city. He had lost sight of the vehicle altogether when he'd stopped for gas. Now; there it was in the desert. The car had returned and the driver was making no secret that they were; in fact, tailing him.

Why had he waited so long to seek out Smoak Tesano? Then again, it wasn't as if he hadn't tried his damndest to get in touch with Hill to let him know what was coming down.

Austin grimaced and slanted another hazel stare toward the rearview. Of course, Hill Tesano made a point of not being easy to find. Next, Austin had tried tracking down Caiphus Tesano but the man proved to be as elusive as his older brother. Things looked promising when he tried making an appointment to see Pike Tesano. Unfortunately, making an appointment was about as far as he'd gotten.

The man had never returned his emails or phone calls. Austin had gone as far as showing up at the offices in New York where Pike handled the philanthropic duties of his grandfather's vast organization. The man was out of the office naturally. Still, Austin vowed to wait until he could be seen.

Pike's staff had been understanding yet firm when they stressed the fact that their boss didn't take kindly to threats, ultimatums, challenges or even suggestions. They hinted that Austin was surely putting his health at risk if he maintained his insistence.

Now, he was attempting a face to face with Smoak Tesano- one who kept as far away from his family as possible. From all Austin had heard, Smoak's personality was about as hospitable as Pike's. Hell, Austin thought, he had to try. He finally accepted the fact that it had been a mistake to try fighting this on his own.

If the gargantuan car in his rear view carried who he suspected, his time was already up. The least he could do

A Lover's Hate

was to warn his friends- *accomplices* about what was in the air.

      The Continental hit his bumper then as if the driver seemed to sense his train of thought in that moment. Austin firmed his grip about the steering wheel. The Hyundai Elantra he drove swerved just slightly when he checked the rear view. Only the hulking car filled the mirror. Austin tried to swallow around the fear in his throat but it was useless. His mouth was as dry as the desert surrounding him.

      The driver of the Continental tapped the Elantra's bumper again and then eased off for a few minutes before starting in once more. Then, the bumper taps were more powerful and sent the Elantra swerving to the other side of the road.

      Austin absently observed the blur of scenery passing the windshield and discovered that he was crying. He didn't criticize himself for it. Past deeds demanded retribution and revenge. That didn't mean he was ready to pay for his crimes with his life.

      Another bumper tap…

      Austin heard a shriek and knew the sound had originated from his throat. Gripping the wheel at that point was a hollow gesture. The circular mechanism swiveled to and fro on its own accord. The car was all over the dusty road.

      A wheel on the Elantra clipped the side of a medium sized boulder; balanced on two wheels momentarily before the front wheel clipped another stone. The small car was thrown into a series of flips until it landed on its roof amidst a flurry of tumbleweeds. Austin was thrown clear of the car. He tried to blink swollen eyes

AlTonya Washington

as disbelief shot through him. He made an attempt to focus on the blur of sky above. He wasn't dead.

Before relief could surge, he saw a shadow and heard the distinct crush of gravel beneath shoe. Correction- he wasn't dead *yet.*

The crushing gravel silenced and the shadow hovered for a time. At last, the figure kneeled.

Austin opened his mouth. Of course, no sound emerged. Still, he tried. No matter the futility of the act, he tried desperately to relay his sorrow to the woman. She was beautiful enough to have been an angel and an angel she was but one of death not of mercy.

"I'm sorry..." his voice came through faint and breaking on fear and the anticipation of his end.

"Shh..."

"I'm so...I'm sor-"

"Shh...I know. I know..." The *angel* stood and waved toward the driver of the Continental.

The car revved rapidly several times before it lurched forward. The powerful vehicle crushed what was left of Austin Chappell's chest. The driver wasn't satisfied and; to ensure the deed was done, reversed the car and drove Austin Chappell deeper into the sun-baked ground. The car shifted gears, and the wheels surged forward to ravage what was left of the lifeless body.

ONE

Las Vegas~ Present…

*D*ammit all. She'd expected- *hoped* to at least have a little
immunity in place when she saw him. Then again, she
hadn't expected to see him there at all. Not in Vegas. Not
on *her* stomping ground. Not where *she* was in control. He
had after all missed his brother's first wedding because
circumstances between the two of them were in a word-
strained.

Yet there he was and there *she* stood unable to keep
the softness of need from her eyes when she turned to face
him. There was no denying it, she knew need was definitely
stirring in her eyes. All she could hope for was that he
didn't see it.

A Lover's Hate

Good luck with that, Sabe. She attempted to swallow and discovered her throat was painfully dry. Hell, she thought, there was no sense denying her need much less trying to hide it. She had always likened Smoak Andreus Tesano to some sort of hybrid wolf adept at tracking its prey. He could probably smell the need all over her.

"Sabra? Are we going to have any problems?" He had repeated his question- his first words to her in about a year.

Where was her voice? Sabra figured it'd be a few minutes more before she'd hunted it down and formulated a response that hopefully wouldn't have her sounding like an idiot. That is...*more* of an idiot than she must have come across standing there and virtually panting for him.

He hadn't changed his cologne once in all the years she'd known him. She wondered if it was some concoction he'd crafted in his desert lab. One designed to drive a woman plumb out of her mind with arousal.

It wouldn't have mattered. Smoak Tesano could accomplish that trick by doing little more than standing just where he was and granting her the delicious opportunity to stare at him. His stance was relaxed, though it would be a mistake for one to think he'd checked his aggression at the door.

His eyes; dark as night and just as bottomless, were truly arresting. His, was a gaze with the power to seduce, intimidate, challenge or freeze in a single, sweeping movement. Partnered with the sexy lift of his mouth; which barely hinted at a smile, the combination gave a woman good reason to stand fixed and desire-filled.

And the bastard knew it, Sabra reminded herself. Smoak Tesano was not a man who played the role of being unaware of his looks, unaware of the advantages they afforded him. He knew exactly how to wield them and his skill was at expert level. The number of times he'd humiliated her should have been a testament to that.

Dammit fool! Speak! She told herself.

"Smoak," she even managed a nod. "Who let you off your leash?"

A corner of his mouth curved upward as if to silently commend the tone she'd selected for their game. "I took myself off," he said.

She rolled her eyes but didn't look away from him. "Still the control freak."

"You seem to like that."

"What do you want?" His comment had prompted her to break eye contact then.

"I want to talk to you."

"Well then," she offered a slight spreading of her hands and waited.

So did Smoak, relaying his meaning in silence as he watched her.

Sabra gritted her teeth, standing in line of the steady glare he'd patented. The look gave away only one hint- he was in no mood to play games. Gathering material from her asymmetrical floor length gown, she stalked past him then, deliberately knocking her shoulder against his. She gave credit to the matching pearl platform pumps that allowed her to do so.

Smoak smiled at the contact and then followed her from the hall.

Sabella Ramsey Tesano bit down on her lip while resting her chin in her palm. From afar, she'd observed the scene between her cousin and her brother-in-law.

"You think it's okay?" She whispered to her husband.

Pike Tesano drained his champagne glass and smirked from his reclining position on the white loveseat he shared with his wife. "She didn't hit him, so I'd say all is well."

Belle eased her husband a skeptical glance and then settled back to snuggle into the curve of his arm. "What do you think he's gonna do?"

"Well," Pike expelled an exaggerated sigh while setting the empty flute to the glass end table flanking the loveseat. "He told me he was gonna have me committed if I let you leave me again."

Belle frowned momentarily, then laughed and let her concerns melt away. The satin folds of her gorgeous gown rustled as she inched up to graze her mouth along the sculpted curve of Pike's jaw.

"So I guess that means you better make me happy then?" She murmured into his smooth bronzed skin.

Pike wasted no further time with pleasantries and hooked his hand about the side of Belle's exquisite pecan brown face. "I plan to give it my very undivided attention Mrs. Tesano."

"You sound very serious Mr. Tesano." Belle could hear her heart thudding in her ears and she shivered from elation.

"Lady you've got no idea."

The newlyweds lost themselves in the most thorough of kisses.

A Lover's Hate

The Ramsey/Tesano wedding had been the stuff of dreams. Virtually no wish had gone unfulfilled. Sabra was of a mind to give her cousin something truly unforgettable and magical. After all, such happiness only visited a chosen few. Sabra was no romantic. Such a gift wasn't in the cards for her, she'd decided. That didn't mean however, that she couldn't live vicariously through Belle's beautiful experience and help to make it as phenomenal as possible.

The room used for the reception teemed with people. It shimmered with an opulence that erred on the side of grace instead of the gaudiness often associated with Vegas. Sabra Ram's was a place of utter beauty, chic sophistication and true sexiness just like its owner.

At that time however, the owner wasn't in much mood to toot her own horn. With Smoak literally at her back, she let the unease claim her expression. He said he wanted to talk, but about what? To that day she had no clue about what went on between them before she woke to find him in her room that morning. To that day she still had *no* desire to find out what had happened.

"Sabra!"

So engrossed in her thoughts, she almost walked by her Beverage Manager Zion Bigelow.

"Sorry to have to do this here," Zion was waving a legal sized clipboard. "Need your name on some final invoices before I head off for my long weekend." He didn't try to mask the excitement over the impending trip.

"Rub it in and I'll change my mind Zy," Sabra threatened in the gruff manner most of her top level employees saw as a pretense. She took the pad in her right hand and signed with her left.

Smoak's faint smile gained definition as he watched her focusing on the invoices and murmuring questions to Zion. God, he wanted her in his life and for more than the yearly battle when they met for contract renegotiations. Long ago, he'd stopped denying that those meetings meant nothing. They were everything to him. He hadn't allowed himself to let go and really touch her since that day when everything changed…it nearly killed him sticking to that promise.

The years between them had only made her stronger and damn if they hadn't made her more provocative. He tuned back into reality then. She was still giving Zion a hard time about his upcoming vacation.

"Gotta keep the wife happy, Sabra."

"Well hell, bring her here. We'll comp y'all up the ying yang. Gia won't ever want to leave." Sabra referred to Zion's wife. She smiled when he laughed, but it was Smoak's clear, low-octave chuckling that sent her heart slamming up into her throat.

Zion shook his head in Smoak's direction. "Always business with this one," he hooked a thumb toward his boss.

"You should be glad, since it allows you to throw away your money on ritzy vacations when you could have one for next to nothing." She finished with the invoices. "Have fun." Her wishes were genuine and she was about to pass the clipboard back to Zion when Smoak intercepted.

Zion froze over the move, knowing his boss's temper all too well. He wondered if the tall dangerous looking man to her right knew what a wildcat Sabra Ramsey could be especially when one saw fit to stick a nose into her business. A frown tugged Zion's bushy,

A Lover's Hate

golden brown eyebrows when he realized his hot-tempered boss had not exploded.

She didn't explode, but her expression said it all. Smoak held the pad in Zion's direction but kept his eyes on Sabra. Challenge and humor lurked in the ebony depths of his gaze as he dared her to retaliate.

Sabra curled fists, but otherwise refused to give into the satisfaction of playing tit for tat. Instead, she actually managed a smile.

"Zion Bigelow, Smoak Tesano. Zion, Smoak's co-owner of the property."

"Well," Zion smiled while sharing a hearty handshake with Smoak. "I didn't know the boss had a partner."

"I don't. Mr. Tesano's interest ends at the land."

"Sabe…" Smoak narrowed his eyes playfully. "You know that's not true."

She blinked, her lips parted in surprise over the comment as well as the look he passed over the length of her body.

Dismissing her reaction, Smoak returned his attention to Zion. "It's good meeting you," he offered another handshake, "have a good time on your trip. Sabe?" he waved, urging her to move along.

Sabra didn't gripe, only set out in search of unoccupied talk space. She thought better of them having the conversation too far away from the crowd. She avoided one of the five elevators in the resort that went all the way to the floor that housed her overflow executive offices and penthouse apartment. There was a small office just off the reception area that would suit their purposes just fine.

AlTonya Washington

Apparently, Smoak disagreed. He closed a hand over her elbow seconds after she passed the elevator.

Sabra freed one of the ties, tamping down her temper, once he'd hustled her into the car. "What the fuck do you think you're doing?" she demanded once the doors whispered shut behind them.

Smoak leaned against the far oak panel of the car. "Don't want us bothered," he loosened the bow tie at his neck.

"Why?" Sabra took refuge against the panel nearest her. "What's so important that it can't wait 'til after your sister-in-law tosses her damn bouquet?"

"Why Sabra," Smoak tilted his head at a curious angle, "I didn't know such things appealed to you."

She raised her chin defiantly. "There's a lot you don't know."

"You're damn right." His gaze shifted toward the elevator control pad, silently instructing her to produce the key needed to send the car to the top of the tower.

Suspicion etched over her lovely dark face a moment longer. Then, she bit the bullet and decided to get the moment behind her.

Brogue Tesano's probing blue stare made a cursory scan of the dim bar. Satisfied that he was the only Tesano (or Ramsey) in the establishment- encouraged him to enter. Still, he chose a seat in the rear and faced the door. Of all the luck, he thought, while flicking a kernel of popcorn to the floor of the otherwise pristine bar on the mezzanine level of Sabra Ram's.

He *would* have to pick the weekend of his cousin's wedding to do this. The gang was all there that was for damn sure. He had to smile then. No one would believe he actually saw beauty in the whole affair. Was he getting soft? Perhaps. But better late than never he supposed and it was definitely late.

Too late? He wondered, raking back strands of honey blonde that persisted in tumbling into a striking face. Yes, it was probably too late, but his explanations were long overdue. Would they change things? He was counting on it. Hopefully, they'd change for the better. Smoak and Sabra would probably have already had their own wedding had it not been for him.

The least he could do was; at long last, tell his cousin that he'd been wrong to blame Sabra. Brogue only hoped he could get Smoak to hear him before the man smashed his face in. Groaning then, he propped his elbows to the table and cradled his face in his hands.

"Now it can't be all *that* bad?"

The sweet voice was attached to a sweet face and even sweeter body. Brogue realized that when he looked out from behind his hands to the petite Asian leaning against his table.

"What would you say if I told you it could be?" he challenged, settling back to appraise the waitress with blatant male appreciation.

She lifted a shoulder beneath the capped sleeved black satin top of her uniform that left her midriff enticingly bare. "I suppose I'd ask if I could make your drink a double."

Brogue chuckled. "Yes, you certainly could," he nodded. "Make it bourbon and keep it comin'."

AlTonya Washington

"Alright…*privacy*. So what the hell is this about and why are we handling paperwork here instead of Phoenix? And where the fuck do you get off takin' over a whole damn floor of my business?"

They were in the private office on the wing opposite the apartment. Smoak leaned against the closed door and hid both hands inside the pockets of his black tuxedo trousers.

"Which question would you like for me to answer first?"

The soft, non-threatening tone of his voice didn't fool her in the least. "Don't screw with my business, Smoak," she sliced the air with an index finger. "I'll fight you. You can sure as shit bet on that."

His smile; the warmth of which, often failed to meet his pitch gaze, was definitely there. Whatever he may have done hadn't taken her fire or her fight. He saw in that instance how strong she was. If he'd ever had any doubts or needed visual proof. He knew however that for all her strength, it wouldn't be enough for what he suspected was coming.

"I'm not here to screw with your business." His voice retained its soft, non-threatening lull. "My people need a place to work is all."

"Why? What's wrong with your lab in Phoenix?"

"What's wrong with my lab in Phoenix is that it's *in* Phoenix. Las Vegas is where I need to be."

"Why?" She didn't care if her voice sounded like a terrified whisper.

Smoak wasn't sympathetic. "Don't play dumb, Sabe. Doesn't suit you."

A Lover's Hate

"Really?" she appeared stunned and vaguely amused then. "I didn't think you believed I had a brain in my head."

Whatever easiness tinged his expression faded. He grimaced, the gesture sharpening already chiseled features and adding something menacing to his very dark face. He regretted every negative aspect of their relationship and the fact that she'd never forget them.

"I apologize Sabra," he spoke quietly, his black stare turned on the floor. "I was dead wrong to ever let you think I believed that."

Her eyelids felt heavy in the wake of sudden weariness. *Don't be nice to me*, she pleaded inwardly. Of course, her toffee stare relayed what she couldn't say. Steeling herself, she prayed for a slow, even voice.

"Just tell me what you want." She managed in the tone she'd summoned.

He nodded in the general direction of the desk. "Maybe you should sit down."

TWO

"I'm fine this way."

Smoak again turned his eyes toward the floor, only this time he smiled. The woman had no idea how hard it was for him to stand there with privacy and opportunity there to be taken advantage of and not *take advantage* of it the way he wanted.

Casting aside the purely X-rated images of things he'd done to her- things they'd done to one another, was a futile move. Every time he looked at her, he wanted her. Her leggy thick frame possessed the kind of curves men dreamed of, fantasized over and often masturbated to. No...the woman had no idea how hard this was for him.

"Do you know a man named Austin Chappell?"

"Austin?" Her surprise was reflected in the response. She'd expected him to say almost anything but that. "Yes, I know him."

"He's dead."

She sat on the edge of her desk. "How?"

"Car accident. Six months ago."

Sabra scanned the floor without really seeing the subtle, intricate patterns in the burgundy and black carpeting. "How do you know this?" She asked finally.

"The accident was pretty bad." Smoak pulled his hands from his pockets and folded his arms over his chest. "It made the news."

Sabra blinked, nodding absently while she absorbed the information. Moments later, she was looking his way again. Suspicion filtered her syrupy stare once again.

"You needed to come all the way up here to tell me that?"

"His crash was no accident. That part didn't make the news." He shrugged. "I've got friends on the force." He contributed the detail. Just how he knew all this would certainly be among her next few questions, he predicted.

The pace of her blinking increased noticeably. Sabra stood, intending to walk the perimeter of her office. She only made it as far as a cream armchair set in the expansive living area of the room. She took a seat on the white oak end table that flanked the chair.

"Why?" Again, her whisper carried the same terrified tone. "You sharing this with me…it's about more than thoughtfulness over the loss of a friend, isn't it?"

Smoak watched her tapping her foot. The front of one pearl pump was just visible beneath the hem of her gown. "How'd you know him?" He asked.

Sabra looked away when Smoak pushed off the door. Her gaze appeared unsettled then for a different reason.

AlTonya Washington

"He was an artist. Did some pieces for the resort. Why are you telling me this, Smoak?" Her eyes had regained some of their suspicious fire. "Do you know who did this?"

Smoak claimed the end table opposite her. "Cops have no leads," he said.

"Do they think someone here-?"

He was already shaking his head. "No clues aside from his travels over the last year or two. The resort popped up and-"

"It was just your civic duty to inform me on the loss of a friend."

The half smile Smoak offered up triggered a line in his cheek that was closer to a splice than a dimple. "Something like that," he said.

The erotic throbbing that had barely ceased inside her, churned back to its former beat. Looking away from him may've brought some relief but naturally that was impossible. Smoak Tesano's face rigid with anger was a picture of unyielding perfection. Soften by compassion; it was utterly indescribable in its magnificence.

Flawless and even toned, his blackberry complexion accentuated the glossy pitch of his hair and eyes. The striking white grin that he rarely shared was an added alluring enhancement.

Somehow Sabra managed to put herself in check-to summon herself out from under whatever spell he cast. Momentarily, she pursed her lips and urged her legs to support her when she stood.

"Well Smoak thanks for thinking enough to tell me about Austin," her words were abrupt, her demeanor guarded.

"Sabra," The half smile was gone. His expression was blank, but for his dark eyes shifting slightly toward the end table.

Sabra resumed her place there. "Now we get to the meat of it," she sighed and let him see her agitation. "I don't appreciate having my time wasted."

"We need to talk about what happened in the bungalow the day you left Phoenix."

"Course we do." Folding her hands over the edges of the table, Sabra braced herself to hear the story she'd run from for a year.

"The woman who came to the door that morning. Did you know her?"

The man had managed to stun her twice in less than thirty minutes.

"The woman...who...came to the door?"

"Did you know her?" He asked as though unmindful of her bewilderment.

She didn't even recall any woman. There had been far more peculiar things that had gone on before anyone came-her eyes slid back to his. "That big bitch," her voice was slow and curious as she remembered.

"Yeah," Gaze soft, Smoak dipped his head a fraction, "she was pretty tall."

"Almost as tall as you and she wasn't wearing any heels."

"Did you ever see her before?"

"I'd have damn well remembered if I had." Sabra blurted, and then braced her hands behind herself on the table. "Why? Is this about what happened to Austin?"

"I don't know, Sweet."

Heat fanned Sabra's cheeks at the smooth, unexpected reminder of how they were together before all

AlTonya Washington

hell broke loose. Sex had been a wild, lusty melding between two partners who gave of their pleasure equally. Images crested to the front of her mind, memories of Smoak whispering his preferred endearment as his mouth worked her into a state of bliss.

Suddenly, she stood again. "I don't know who she was," she told him with a singular decisive wave, "and if that's all you want out of me then I'm sorry I can't help you. I have a reception to oversee in case you forgot." She looked down to fluff the hem of the gown where it had gathered about her pumps.

Smoak took his time about standing and Sabra wanted to punch him for appearing so cool and unruffled while she feened for him. He finally came to his feet and moved toward her. She forbid herself to retreat, praying he couldn't hear her relieved sigh when his steps slowed and then halted.

He didn't rush working his stare up the length of her body. "Thank you for giving me your time," he said once his appraisal was complete.

His words could have made her moan. She commanded herself to resist the urge until he was gone.

"I'll see you later, alright?"

Her desire to moan- waned…"What for?"

Smoak had pulled the loosened tie from his collar and was shoving it into his back pocket. "We've got business concerning the construction."

"Of?"

His grin held no humor. "Jesus your memory's short."

"What-?"

"My lab."

"You're serious?"

"Did you really think I was joking?"

"At least a joke wouldn't have me thinking you're a complete idiot." Kicking at the confining hem of the gown, she closed a measure of the distance between them. "You can't have your chemistry set behind my casino Smoak. Even for Vegas, that's just *too* weird."

He turned for the door. "We'll discuss it."

"I won't have it."

Leaving was forgotten. Smoak took a slow scan of the plush office before setting his glare to Sabra. "You'll either have *it* or you'll have one hell of a fight on your hands."

Sabra didn't lash out at the threat. Instead, she studied him as if he were a puzzle she was trying to solve.

"That weirdo at the bungalow and what happened to Austin...are you concerned for my safety, Smoak?" Silently she called herself a fool. Her safety was the last thing he cared about.

Smoak didn't confirm nor deny her curiosity. Moreover, his expression gave nothing away. "You don't want to get on my bad side about this. You've had free reign over this land since the day we got it."

"I never asked you to let me have it."

"But you didn't turn down my offer, did you? You took everything I gave and you didn't complain once."

Sabra looked away then but didn't relinquish her stance. His words carried so many meanings she'd be a babbling idiot by the time he left. Regardless, she wasn't about to turn tail and run. Pulling steel into her eyes, she sauntered a few steps closer.

"I won't let you take my business, Smoak. I'll fight you, buy you out, step in any mud pit you want to roll around in but you won't take my business." Her glare was scathing in its evaluation. "At least I did something with the land. Left to you, it would've just blended in with the rest of the desert."

"And you've got plenty of uncultivated property that'll suit my purposes just fine." He massaged the sleek hair tapered at his nape and put a faint smile in place. "This doesn't have to be ugly, Sabe."

She was working up a rebuttal when he placed an index finger across her mouth to silence her.

"We'll talk about it later, alright?" He grazed his thumb across her parted lips and was slow to look away or remove his fingers. "We should get back before everyone starts thinking we're killing each other up here." His eyes lingered on her face. "Thanks for hearing me out, Sweet."

Sabra waited for the door to close at his back. "But you didn't tell me anything." She whispered to the empty room.

***

Imani Tesano had enjoyed every minute of her son's remarriage to the woman he'd never stopped loving. The only thing that could have made her happier would have been to see all her sons settled with the women they loved. While that miracle would've made her happier, it wouldn't have been alone in its power to do so. Imani discovered that when her third son twirled her chair around and kissed her full on the mouth.

Gleeful tears pooled Imani's dark eyes when she looked into Smoak's darker ones. She sighed, smoothing her hands across his broad shoulders before cupping his face.

"My love," her voice trembled as she pulled him close for another kiss.

"I'm sorry for not getting over to you sooner," Smoak hugged his mother tight, inhaling her scent and drawing contentment from it. "When I got here you were in a crowd and then I saw Sabra and…"

"She's who you really came to see."

Smoak didn't try putting on airs for his mother. It was useless anyway. The woman could see through him so easily it was almost eerie. He noted that Sabra was quickly grasping the art of that same skill.

"I shouldn't be here, but I had to come."

"Of course you did." Imani grazed the back of her hand across her son's jaw. "I think you're finally ready to walk in your brother's footsteps."

Smoak's laughter; when he chose to share it was deep, honest and totally without guile.

"You know Pike's courage comes from some insane place." He told his mother.

A light sent Imani's eyes twinkling a little more brilliantly. "Insanity and happiness often come from the same place." She gave a little shrug. "When love's to blame, there's nothing better."

"We're volatile together, Mama." Faint sparkles of foreboding illuminated his eyes. "Sabra and me-we…I've never done right by her. Even before I…hurt her the way I did…I was so caught up in my own drama. Hating the family…"

"Shh…" Imani smoothed her hand over his hair.

"I let them make me hate myself and I took it out on her."

"And still she loves you."

"Maybe she shouldn't."

"Maybe she sees in you what you refuse to see in yourself."

"I hurt her, Mama." He squeezed his eyes shut for a few seconds. "You know I did-"

"Shh…I think she'll accept your apology if only you let your guard down enough to give it."

Smoak shook his head like a defiant boy. "I don't want to screw up with her again, Mama. I rather be without her than do that." He said, even though *being without her* was something he didn't have the strength to maintain.

"She's not as tough as she makes out. Belle told me that, but I already knew it. All that attitude she wears, it's not her- not all of it."

"So don't you think that means you should stay close to her instead of keeping your distance?"

Smoak didn't answer. That's why he was there, wasn't it? As for the rest, the intimate dramas between them…would she take him at his word if he told her she was all he'd ever wanted? That he'd literally mourned the loss of what they could've had if he hadn't let his demons get in the way?

"There he is!"

Imani and Smoak looked up to see Roman heading toward them. Smoak and his mother shared a meaningful smile, then he kissed her again and stood to greet his father.

It was often said that if Roman Tesano wanted to look into a mirror, he need only seek out his third son. Minus the sleek onyx complexion, Smoak was almost the exact devastating replica of his father.

The two men embraced. Roman took time to cup his son's face and take his own parental inventory just as Imani had done moments earlier. Seeming satisfied, he gave Smoak's cheek a playful slap.

"We're about to get started."

"Right," Smoak sighed in reference to his father's reminder. "Tenth floor conference room."

"A few are already up there." Roman said.

"I'm on my way." Smoak leaned down to press a kiss into Imani's neck. "I'll see you later," he murmured into her skin and then set off.

Roman observed his son's departure and then knelt by his wife's wheelchair. "He okay?"

"Pining for the woman he loves and too terrified to bare his soul and beg her forgiveness."

Roman nuzzled his face against Imani's temple. "I'm glad I have you to put all the guys' love dramas into perspective for me. I've never been able to keep up."

Imani's laughter sounded as regal as her voice. "They do lead intriguing love lives."

"Wonder where they get it."

"Ah well…they *are* their father's sons."

Roman clutched his chest as if pained. "Please don't put that on me." He brushed his thumb near the corner of Imani's eye before he kissed her there. "I won't be long. Want me to take you to the room first?"

"No. Our daughter-in-law won't toss the bouquet until you're done with this meeting, so hurry."

"Understood," Roman nodded dutifully and then moved in for a more suitable kiss. It was only to be a quick peck to the mouth, but it lasted a tad longer than expected. Roman's dark eyes smoldered with adoration for his wife. Then, he stood, tweaked her chin and was gone.

Lee Lee Arnold had run every errand and put out almost every fire imaginable. There was only one endeavor she couldn't quite square away. For every five waitresses, dancers or office staff; whom she assured had *no* chance with any of the Ramsey or Tesano men, five more in each category seemed to crop up with more sly inquiries about the sexy brood gracing Sabra Ram's with their presence.

Lee Lee was on her way to the bar for a needed and well-deserved drink. Half way to her destination, she was jerked back and almost out of her strappy petal pink heels.

"Dammit Sabra!" she hissed when she saw who had grabbed her arm. "What the-"

Sabra jerked Lee Lee's arm again, seconds after the woman had managed to tug it free. "I need you to put them back on." Her gaze was focused, her tone direct as she spoke the request.

Lee Lee was still tending to her arm. Sabra's grip was like a vice.

"Lee Lee."

"What?"

"I need you to put them back on."

"Right. What?" Lee Lee finally looked at her friend. Sabra merely waited, watching her with a knowing intensity. Lee Lee understood. She was about to shake her head when Sabra hugged her face in both hands.

"Do it." She ordered.

"No." Lee Lee pulled at Sabra's hands while making a valiant attempt at shaking her head. When she finally succeeded in breaking free, she tugged Sabra with her to a semi-private corner.

"What is this? What's happened?"

"Dammit Lee! Just once can't you do what the fuck I tell you without all the questions?"

"You don't need them. We agreed-"

"Then I'm breakin' the agreement."

"What's happened?" Lee's slanting hazel stare began an intense survey, looking Sabra up and down. "Why are you asking for them? Is this about Smoak?"

Sabra closed her eyes as if defeated and Lee Lee had her answer. She'd had her suspicions when Smoak had acquired the space in the first tower. Still, she refused to think it would come back to this...

"Lee please," Sabra's voice resembled a wounded moan.

"Alright honey," Lee Lee's fair delicate face was soft with sympathy. "Alright I'll put them on but we won't use them."

"But I-"

"Shh...Let's try it this way, okay? You've been doing so well."

Sabra blinked away the water fringing her lashes. "I'm scared." She admitted, squeezing Lee Lee's hands as if to draw strength. "I need you to take care of it."

"I'll do it Sabra, but we *won't* use them. Not yet. Understood?"

Sabra knew her friend wouldn't budge farther from her original decision. She nodded. "Then you'll have to be there. You'll have to be there Lee." She insisted.

"I will Hon," Lee Lee drew Sabra's trembling frame into a hug and held on tight. "I swear I'll be there."

THREE

Conversation was steady but quiet in the 10th floor conference room of the second tower. All the attendees had not yet arrived in the split level room. Among those who were there, discussion centered around the obvious mystery surrounding the upcoming meeting.

Fernando would be a no show as he was still enjoying his honeymoon with Contessa. His brothers, Yohan and Moses took their places at opposite ends of a long cushioned sill that ran the length along the window that looked down on the ninth green of the resort's eighteen-hole golf course.

Reclining in a gray leather swivel, Taurus took residence in one of the thirty chairs at the glass rectangular table. The twins shared one of the room's four gray leather sofas. The Tesanos had not yet arrived.

"What the fuck is this shit?" Quay's voice rang out over the sports talk going back and forth between Moses and Yohan.

"Maybe we're here to organize a send-off for the newlyweds." Quest's tone relayed his weariness while he slouched on his end of the sofa and massaged his eyes.

Moses grunted a laugh and rested his shaved head back against the window. "That's a good guess but I think our new cousin-in-law is on this guest list too."

"Shit," Quay muttered, leaning forward to brace his elbows to his knees while smoothing his palm over a clenched fist.

"Anybody want a drink?" Yohan left his spot on the sill.

"Hell yeah," Taurus sighed.

"Second," Moses agreed.

Quest raised two fingers to request that Yohan add him and his twin to the drink tally.

The door lever turned just then and Smoak walked into the room.

"Well, well, the black sheep."

"Quay," Quest softly reprimanded and shook his head over his brother's remark.

Smoak didn't appear to take offence to Quaysar's slur. He moved into the room to shake hands with the guys. To Quay, he merely nodded.

"Any idea what the hell we're doin' here, man?" Yohan asked in the midst of pouring Hennessey for the group.

Smoak grimaced and tossed his jacket over the back of a chair. "Not a clue. All my dad said was where to be and when to be here."

"And how is it that *you're* here?"

"Quay."

"Fuck that, Q." Quay waved a hand at Quest but kept his gaze trained on Smoak. "Your brother's weddings ain't exactly your cup of tea, are they?"

Smoak's stance remained as cool as his expression. "Maybe I'm tryin' to make up for that."

"*Bullshit*," Quay sang in a mocking tone.

"Jesus..." Quest groaned and left the sofa. He intercepted the glass Yohan was about to hand over to Taurus.

"Admit it." Quay didn't see the need to let up on Smoak. "You're really here to see Sabra."

Smoak's smile held a cunning intent. "Damn Quay, guess I should've told you a long time ago. I've seen your cousin every year since we broke up."

The reference to that particular point in time cut the final tie on Quay's dangerous temper and he made a move for Smoak. Both men were more than ready to go at it. For Quaysar, it was simply a matter of standing up for his cousin. Smoak's reasoning went a bit deeper.

He was fueled by his own self-loathing over his part in the matter. He missed Sabra in the most basic way. Frustration simmered over being summoned to a meeting when he wanted to be with the woman he loved, protecting her and trying to find a way back into her heart.

Emotions ran icy hot and heavy on both sides, laying the foundation for a vicious exchange. Yohan's quick reflexes and sheer massiveness, doused the raging flames when he stepped between the two men squaring off. He shoved Quay to the sofa and pushed Smoak back a foot and a half.

Quest returned to the sofa. He took a seat on the arm next to Quay and put a hand on his brother's shoulder. "You have to understand how curious we are about why you're here after all this time. If I'm not mistaken, Sabra goes to Phoenix for your meetings about the land, right?"

Smoak only lowered his head a fraction to serve as a response to Quest. "Thanks, man." He said to Yohan who had just set a glass of liquor into his hand.

"So?" Moses prompted when there was no further explanation from Smoak. "What the hell are you doin' here? The girl's been on pins and needles about you showin' up since you took over the top floor on the other side." His dark eyes narrowed sharply as they probed. "My guess is she wouldn't have turned down the chance to handle your business in Arizona and leave you there."

"It's got nothing to do with signing contracts for the resort." Smoak shared the information and then savored a swig of the liquor.

Quay was ready to leave the sofa again but took heed of the warning squeeze Quest applied to his shoulder. "So you've just been wasting my wife's time building some monstrosity to cart your black ass around whatever you told her you were tryin' to build out here?"

"Quay I promise I'm not wasting Tykira's time and I'm not here to cause trouble for Sabra." Smoak directed the second portion of the statement toward Moses.

"So?" Taurus inquired that time. "You haven't answered Mo's question. What's this visit about?"

Smoak finished his drink. "Y'all are just gonna have to trust me." He said when he was done.

"*Fuck that,*" Quay used the mocking tone again to sing the phrase.

AlTonya Washington

Quest grimaced at his twin. "Man you gotta know we can't do that without good reason." He said.

Smoak nodded, understanding the concern. He decided it couldn't hurt to be a little more forthcoming.

"Guys I honestly don't know what I've got- just a bunch of hunches."

"Which can often lead to the full story," Taurus noted, his extraordinarily light gaze was fixed and unreadable.

Resigned, Smoak shrugged. "I may know more once I talk to my dad and my brother."

"Hill," Quest guessed.

Again, Smoak shrugged his confirmation. "Six months ago an artist by the name of Austin Chappell was killed. He knew Sabra-did some work for her here at the resort. His death wasn't an accident. Six months before that- the day Sabra was set to leave after our meeting, she got a visit from a woman she didn't know. The woman obviously knew who she was and that woman was obviously disturbed. Combine that with the fact that certain Tesanos want me on the payroll and have been calling Sabra to…draw me in …it's all just a little too strange not to be connected somehow."

The five Ramseys in the room straightened as their interest peaked.

"You think the woman was connected to this Chappell's death?" Yohan asked.

"It's possible." Smoak went to the bar for a refill.

"Who do you think she was?" Quay asked. He was more interested then, in what Smoak had to say than in making him look bad.

"I don't know who she was." Smoak paused at the bar instead of reaching for the bottle of brown liquor. "She just looked…wrong. Acted almost like a child at times which is funny 'cause she was tall as fuck." He massaged the back of his neck and then smirked. "I'd bet everything I own that she was psychotic."

"So was her visit personal to Sabra or do you think it was about more? Be straight with us, man." Quay quietly insisted.

Smoak forgot his drink and fixed Quay with an acknowledging smile. "Until six months ago, I wondered about that very thing."

"Until the artist's death?" Moses guessed.

"Nothing fits." Smoak let them see his bewilderment and his agitation. "It makes no sense for it all to be connected, but I know it is."

"Christ…" Quest hissed.

"Q…" Quay called in a warning that mocked his brother's earlier tone.

"So we were idiots to think this shit was on its way to a close?"

Smoak couldn't respond to Quest.

"You're here to protect her, aren't you?" Yohan asked.

"Yes." Smoak's reply to that question came without reservation. Again, he let the men in the room see his bewilderment. "But protect her from what? I haven't got a clue."

Pike was finally able to pull himself away from his bride and head up for the meeting his father had called. Anyone who'd had the unfortunate luck to brush up against his bad side over the last several years may have been just as unsettled by the smile that softened the angles of his

AlTonya Washington

darkly provocative features then. The smile of course was going nowhere, for the desire to do so came from someplace deep and finally at peace within.

He was waiting for the elevator to arrive in the mini-bay off a remote corridor from the reception hall. He actually hummed to the bass thrumming in the air, courtesy of the jazz band that had relieved the DJ who had been spinning a mix of 80s and 90s Hip Hop. His smile only deepened when a gruff, familiar voice caught his ear.

"Let her leave you again and I'll kill you."

Pike's contented smile turned into a cocky grin. He turned to the tall, heavily muscled man who stood a couple of feet down the hall.

"Your little brothers only threatened to have me committed." Pike said.

Hilliam Tesano barely shrugged. "What's the fuckin' good in that?"

Quiet rumbling laughter broke out between the brothers and they met for a tight embrace.

"Good job, Chump." Hill murmured into his brother's neck and planted a kiss there.

"Thanks," Pike's voice muffled in Hill's shoulder as he squeezed him tight. "Glad you're here."

Hill's very deep-set gaze was sharper when he pulled back to survey his younger brother. "But I'm *not* here." He cautioned.

Pike nodded, understanding, "Will you at least see Mama before you vanish?"

The wide set of Hill's mouth thinned into a grimmer line. "I *have* seen her."

"Talked to her?"

"You know I can't."

"Still?"

A Lover's Hate

"Until I make this right."

Pike muttered an obscenity. "You've got nothing to make right," he whispered.

Hill smirked and reached out to straighten the black handkerchief peeking from the front pocket of Pike's tux. "You know that's not true." His voice held an easy timber.

"So what are you doin' here, then?" Pike couldn't help but snap.

Hill only smiled more broadly. "Wanted to know what dad's meeting was about."

"How did-"

"The Rugrat."

Pike smiled. Hill rarely referenced any of them by name unless they'd royally pissed him off. He'd always been the Chump, Smoak was the Kid and Caiphus was the Rugrat.

"So you just happened to be in Vegas when he called, huh?"

Hill shrugged again, bringing a crinkle to the silver gray fleece hoody he sported. The smile softening his face took on a wicked glint. "Had to make sure you didn't try to punk out of walkin' down the aisle." He mussed Pike's hair and laid a playful slap on his cheek.

"So listen, it won't do for too many folks to see us all together just yet, you know?" Hill scanned the hallway briefly. "We're supposed to be on the outs, remember?"

"Where will you be?" Pike asked.

"Got a suite here. The Rugrat knows where. He'll tell you guys when it's cool."

"Good," Pike nodded as though relieved. "Belle'll kill me if I'm not back for her to toss the bouquet."

"And so she should." Hill pulled his brother into another hug. "And so she should," he repeated.

AlTonya Washington

***

Westin Ramsey clapped Moses' shoulder and stepped out of the conversation he'd been having with him, Taurus and Yohan. He'd spotted Caiphus Tesano arriving in the conference room that had been steadily filling for the last ten minutes.

"Mr. Ramsey," Caiphus' smile was genuine, reaching the brilliant turquoise depths of his eyes. "Good to see you," he added when they met for handshakes.

"Same here," Westin returned the sentiment and leaned into a brief hug while they still clutched hands.

"Will you tell tales out of school and give a hint as to what this meeting's about?"

"No idea, son…" Westin played the obvious innocent, though pure devilry lurked in his features which were sharper and more striking with the onset of age.

Caiphus rolled his eyes, not buying any of the act. "I know you five still share everything," he referred to Westin, Damon, Roman, Pitch and Aaron.

"How's your uncle?" Westin asked, speaking of Aaron Tesano whose illness of late had prevented him from attending the wedding.

"He's a tough old bird," Caiphus smiled on the thought of the man. "I think his doctors just want him to get a little more rest."

"Good luck with them convincing him to do that." Westin chuckled.

"Hmph…you're not gonna tell me a damn thing, are you?" Caiphus acknowledged.

"Not a damn thing," Westin clapped the younger man's shoulder. "At least you have the luxury of getting answers to your questions momentarily. Meanwhile, I'm still hoping for a few scraps of info about the moves my daughter's making in that godforsaken job of hers."

Caiphus sighed. It was the usual turn of discussion whenever he spoke with Sybilla Ramsey's father. Understandably, the man had always been concerned and terrified over the fact that his only daughter- only child made her living in a profession that often put her face to face with the world's most abominable souls.

Caiphus didn't like it either. Over the years, he used his considerable resources to keep her as safe as possible. He'd managed to do a decent job, but Sybilla was tough to manage. The woman definitely didn't take kindly to being protected.

"I promise you it's alright, sir." Caiphus dropped a hand to Westin's shoulder. "She's got a good crew around her."

"But she's still in the line of too many fires."

"Sir, you have to believe I'm doing everything in my power to keep her safe." Caiphus shook his head and let only a hint of his abundant frustration show. "She's so damn stubborn, sir." He confessed.

Westin's grimace faltered with traces of amusement rising. "Like her mother…"

"She *is* strong, though."

"As strong as she thinks?" Westin countered.

Caiphus could only respond with a resigned smile. Westin seemed satisfied and threw his head back to laugh.

Along one end of the corridor outside the conference room, Roman stood in conversation with his brother Pitch and Damon Ramsey.

"How much you plan on tellin' them?" Damon asked.

"Probably nothin' they wouldn't find out on their own if they keep diggin'." Roman said.

"And you're sure they're diggin'?"

"Aren't you?" Roman challenged his friend. "Quest is now at the helm of Ramsey. He's just shut down a powerful arm of the company- a corrupt arm, but a powerful one. I'm guessing Marc and Houston kept some pretty creative records."

Damon smoothed a hand across the dark hair tapered at his neck. "I tried keepin' as close an eye on those fools as I could. But in weapons…they had a lot of loyalty over there."

"And now Quest has broken it down- they'd have found some link to this sooner or later too. Hell D, they all know what Marc was into with Charlton- the girls, the trafficking, the whole ovary… sickness…"

"And you think telling them this Dr. Ferrat's story will get 'em to stop asking questions?"

Roman shook his head. "Just the opposite. I've spent decades tryin' to uncover what those kids found in less than a few years." He raked a hand through his thick, silky hair. "This is about pooling my resources. Maybe they'll latch onto something we've overlooked. Whatever madness my brother Humphrey started, is still goin' on. Maybe our boys can find a way to bring it down."

"Could work," Damon said and then rolled his eyes and massaged the bridge of his nose. "Or it could open up a whole new can of worms. You sure about this?"

"There's peace in your family for the first time in how long?"

A Lover's Hate

Damon's smile triggered both his dimples. "In ever."

Roman shrugged. "I want that for my sons- especially Smoak. He would've been ruined if I hadn't gotten him away from them and all that...hatred."

"And Grekka?" Pitch spoke up then, referring to their older brother Gabriel Tesano. "Will you tell them what he did?"

"They already suspect- with confirmation they'd kill him." Roman predicted as his features hardened. "And that pleasure is for me."

FOUR

Sabra was of a mind to hide out in her apartment for the rest of the event. She'd have one of her staff call up when Belle was ready to throw her flowers and then she'd make a mad dash back down to the reception. No one would be the wiser. The day had been draining and in more ways than one. She needed time alone or else she'd scream.

I'm gonna scream, Sabra sang to herself when she silenced her mind's inner ramblings and realized she was heading directly for her mother.

Georgia Ramsey stood statuesque in an ice blue gown with an upturned collar and deep split. She was chic, lovely and similar to a queen surveying her world. Sabra had to hand it to the woman; Georgia could stake her claim without saying a word. Of course, Georgia Ramsey never did anything without saying a word.

Sabra had only a minute to redirect her course without being seen. Instead, she made the subconscious decision to go on and meet her fate.

"Hey Mommy," she sighed and waited on some sort of criticism.

The cool look Georgia wore never faded. Sabra felt her eyes narrowing in surprise as she examined her mother's face. The woman almost appeared pleasant.

"Are you okay, darling?" Georgia asked, having noticed her daughter's leery expression.

"Um…well yeah…are you?" Sabra's surprise bordered on shock when Georgia actually laughed.

"I'm wonderful darling."

"Really?" Sabra almost croaked the word.

Georgia didn't appear to tune into her daughter's amusement. "Must be the atmosphere. You've done a spectacular job here, love."

Disbelief settled in amongst Sabra's other emotions. She stood ordering her mouth not to fall open and listened to Georgia rave. The woman didn't voice one criticism.

"Babygirl!"

Sabra felt all her uncertainties and apprehensions melt away at the sound of her father's voice. Felix Cade's looks and casually charming manner were as potent as they'd ever been. Sabra couldn't help but wonder how many phone numbers the man had pocketed from all the women who had surely gotten lost beneath his spell. She threw her arms about his neck and laughed.

"How's my Babygirl?" Felix's voice rumbled.

Sabra squeezed him tight. "Just fine now, daddy," she closed her eyes contentedly.

Felix set her away after a few seconds and studied her face. "You look tired."

"It's been a long day," she fixed her eyes on the satiny black lapel of his tux. "Lots of preparations…"

"Our daughter's done a fantastic job, Felix."

Sabra let her mouth fall open then. *Wait a minute*, she thought; were these her parents- her *mother* being sweet? Doting? Yes, it had definitely been a long day.

Felix tugged his daughter into another hug. "You get some rest after all this is finished, alright?"

Sabra nodded against his shoulder. "I promise, daddy." She stepped back then and observed yet another in a series of strange events.

"Dance with me Georgie?" Felix was asking.

Georgia placed her hand in her ex-husband's palm and practically floated away with him.

***

"Gentlemen, looks like we're all here. Let's get started."

The rumble of Pitch Tesano's voice caught everyone's attention and they acted accordingly. Damon Ramsey took a spot on the back of the sofa occupied by his twin sons. Moses and Yohan maintained their places at the window sill with Taurus at the long conference table. Westin perched at one corner of the table as well. Caiphus and Pike occupied the deep armchairs near the door while Smoak leaned next to Pitch against the wall. Everyone's eyes were turned toward Roman who stood near the center of the room, affording him a view of every man in attendance.

"Thank you all for coming. My wife told me to make this quick and I'm sure everyone has more enjoyable things to do-especially the groom." Roman slanted a wink at his son and the men spared a few seconds of applause for Pike.

"I'll go on and apologize now," Roman slipped his hands into his pockets and bowed his head. "What I need to say is going to put a damper on the happiness of the day but; as there's probably a one in a trillion chance that we'll all be in the same place at the same time any time soon, this was the best opportunity."

"Opportunity for what, Dad?" Smoak asked, observing the drawn look coming to his father's face.

"Many years ago, I had reason to suspect that some of my brothers were involved in something heinous. Turned out I was right. What I didn't know was that it all started long before I ever even suspected. Before some of you were even born." Roman paused to rub his fingers against the side of his nose.

"I still don't have all the answers, but what I *have* uncovered was recently confirmed by a qualified source. I'm coming to you all now because there's strength in numbers and I hope you'll catch something I've overlooked."

"This is a surprise, Dad." Pike spoke up then. "I'd think you wouldn't want us pokin' around in anything related to…that side of the family."

"I don't." Roman admitted, and then rolled his eyes while he shrugged. "Guess it's my jealousy taking over. West and Damon finally have real peace in their family and I want the same for us."

"Sir," Quest raised his hand and then waved it around the room, "what's this got to do with us?"

"Right," Roman nodded, "I'll make this as quick as I can."

***

AlTonya Washington

All areas of Sabra Ramsey's resort reflected the appeal of classic luxury. No place reflected that more than the Courtyards of Sabra Ram's. The exquisite indoor havens harbored the beauty of the outdoors. Foliage and flowers bloomed like greenhouse plants year round and smelled like fragrant meadows. Two of the four 'havens' were constructed as a series of intricate mazes at the east and west wings of the first tower. Fully stocked bars were established at the entrances and center of each courtyard.

Sybilla and Briselle Ramsey had escaped the hubbub of the reception. They stole away for a quiet drink and walk about the man-made grounds.

"Thanks for suggesting this." Bill told her mother, hugging her close as they strolled arm in arm.

Briselle smiled and rested her temple next to Sybilla's. "I wasn't sure whether this would interest you. I'm sure it's a little slow for your pace."

"Mmm…" Bill let her lashes flutter dreamily. "That's why it's so nice."

"How are you, Baby?"

Bill didn't mind the question. Her mother was the only one who ever made her feel like she could do… anything.

"There's something new stirring at work. Looks like it'll have me busier than ever."

"I see…so you'll be out in the field again then?"

Bill heard the concern in Bri's voice. "I think so." She gave her mother's arm a reassuring squeeze when the woman sighed. "I've done it many times, Mama."

"I know," Bri patted her hand. "And I know you can handle it, little girl."

A Lover's Hate

Bill laughed shortly and looked over at her mother in wonder. "How can you call me 'little girl' and make me feel like superwoman at the same time?"

"Oh…" Briselle's light eyes sparkled as she looked up at the vibrant vines towering and twisting overhead. "It's a gift we moms have. You'll see when you have a little one of your own." She looked over in time to see the doubt shadowing Bill's fine-boned face.

Bill knew what her mother was thinking and *who* she was thinking about. "I think we're gonna bump up against each other in this new assignment. It's confusing." She admitted. "I've spent a long time thinking the worst of Caiphus and now I may have been wrong."

"Oh honey," Briselle's exquisite features were radiant with excitement.

"Hold your horses, Miss Bri." Sybilla shook her head. "I may've been wrong about him professionally. Personally, I've been dead on."

"Are you so sure Miss Globetrotting Special Agent?" Bri challenged. "You've got all the facts? No mistakes? No misjudgments?"

"Not about that, Ma. Please tell me you haven't forgotten the way he used our relationship to tarnish my image with Lamont? I could've gotten fired over that."

Briselle's laughter was closer to the giggle of a small girl. "Your father would've loved that!"

Sybilla wasn't amused.

"Oh honey…" Bri pulled her daughter down with her to a polished white bench. "Don't you think he could've been trying to protect you instead of hurt you?" She tapped Bill's chin with her index finger when she bristled. "I know you don't like the word, but the man is in love with you."

"Past tense, Mama."

"I don't think so, Baby." Bri pretended to pull a green sprig from the cuff of the peach chiffon blazer worn over a swing dress of the same color. "I saw you together talking at the reception. When you walked away he was still staring after you."

"Dang skippy he was. I look *good* in this pantsuit." Bill teased and joined her mother in laughter.

"That too, but there's more." Bri said when her laughter tapered. "When you get over your anger at what he did and why you *think* he did it, maybe you'll be able to see that." She kissed Bill's forehead and gave her arm a tug. "Now come on, I heard Sabra's got a manmade waterfall somewhere in here."

"Does this Dr. Ferrat remember anything about where she worked?" Smoak was asking after his father had shared the story of the meeting with the intelligent yet eccentric Madeline Ferrat. "If we could get a location- even if it's no longer operational, maybe that'd be a starting point."

Roman exchanged a discouraging look with Pitch who turned to address his nephew.

"Madeline made a point of discussing how elaborate everything was, how Hump came off like he had more money than God. To make a very long story even longer, they were carried to and from their place of business via submarine."

Hushed rounds of flagrant curses filled the room then.

"Are you serious?" Moses challenged, a half smile of disbelief on his darkly gorgeous face.

A Lover's Hate

"How is that possible?" Smoak's voice was quiet and carried on equal disbelief as his eyes narrowed to glinting black slits.

"She saw it." Pitch grinned at the reactions. From a sleeve of the portfolio he'd brought to the conference room, he withdrew an old Polaroid. In the worn picture was a young Madeline Ferrat waving as she stood near a black vessel which sat next to what looked like a pier. The fuselage left no confusion as to what the vessel was.

"She took the picture on the sly," Roman shared. "Charmed one of the deck hands into doing it."

"And if you ever met Madeline you'd know she could charm the devil into handin' over his own pitchfork." Pitch qualified.

Roman smiled and then nodded toward Pike. "Got somethin' on your mind son?"

"I just think we might be spinnin' our wheels here, Dad. I mean," he leaned forward and began to tick the points off on his fingers. "Uncle Hump's dead. They've found…Marc's remains. Houston's gone, so is Muhammad. How do you know the whole organization isn't on its last legs anyway?"

"I know because so many of the family's…other dealings are still in motion. Not to mention the fact that certain members of my family saw fit to get rid of those who went behind their backs to turn over secrets. They go after strangers as coolly as they go after family."

"What are you sayin' Dad?" Smoak left the wall to sit on the arm of Caiphus' chair.

"Your Uncle Stone was killed on Humphrey's order. Stone was having second thoughts about whatever the hell they'd gotten into." Roman gave the younger men time to absorb the information. "This was part of

Madeline's story and I know enough about my family to know it's true."

"But Dad, how does that tell you this is still going on?" Pike persisted.

Roman passed an exasperated look to Pitch, who shrugged.

"Guess you're right. Rome. They'll find out anyway."

The group was rapt with curiosity as they waited, watching Roman pacing the room as he debated.

"When I got too close to turning over the rock covering this ugly mess, I was...*asked* to step back. They *asked* by running my car off the road, but it wasn't me in the truck that day."

Smoak, Caiphus and Pike stood at once. Their faces harbored triple expressions of rage.

"You finally confirmed it." Smoak's tone was as venomous as his gaze.

"On Gabe's order?" Pike's voice was void of tone or emotion.

"Dad." Caiphus' gaze bored holes into his father.

Pitch moved closer to the circle, fearing his brother might need assistance holding back the angry trio.

Roman needed no help. "You three listen to me, I won't say it again. Gabriel is mine-for me to handle- to seek out." He stepped closer to give each of his sons the benefit of a stare as hard and black as obsidian.

"You'll disappoint me very much if you go over my head on this."

The soft warning was all too effective. Pike, Smoak and Caiphus knew their father well enough to know how severe the consequences of disappointing him could be.

"Dad," Smoak risked stepping even closer, "we understand what you're saying but you can't just tell us they tried to kill her and not expect us to do anything about it."

"I don't expect that at all," Roman brought a hand to Smoak's shoulder and squeezed. "I expect you to pick up or continue on wherever your private investigations lead you. Seeing this to the end was important for me, but I've found enough. I'm going to kill my brother." He nodded once to relay the certainty of that to his sons. "I'll take great pleasure in doing so. Your mother needs me and I-I've been so consumed by hate over what happened to her that I haven't given her the best of me. She deserves that."

Roman beckoned Caiphus and Pike to move in. "Gabriel will be a non-entity soon but you know Vale is ten times more depraved than he or Humphrey and they taught him well. Whatever this shit is, you can best believe he's still in the middle of it. You'll need to work together to bring it down. *All* of you. You need to squash whatever unrest you've got goin' on and handle this."

Across the room, Damon slapped the back of Quay's head in warning.

Roman turned to address the crowd then. "You're family men. None of you want this hanging over your lives and it surely will, just as it has over ours." He looked from Pitch to Westin and Damon. "That's all guys. Not as short as I promised, but..." he shrugged.

Soft conversation and the hint of laughter began to fill the room as some of the tension lifted. Smoak was huddled with his brothers when Quaysar walked up and pushed against his shoulder.

Smoak's expression was unreadable when he saw Quay and he waited on the man's next move. Pike's,

Caiphus' and Quest's jaws dropped when Quay extended a hand to shake with Smoak.

"Sorry," Quay said with a lopsided grin.

"Understood," Smoak accepted the shake. "I'd be suspicious of my motives too."

"Should we be?" Quay asked.

"I swear I'm not here to hurt her. I've done enough of that and I'll never be able to make up for it." Smoak grimaced and then sighed. "I'd just settle for the chance to try."

Quay nodded slowly. "Fair enough."

"Well good," Quest said once he felt the happy vibes had lingered long enough. "Now that we're all friends again, were you guys workin' with Hill on this already? Was it just a cover so nobody would suspect y'all were workin' together toward the same end?"

"Jesus," Caiphus sounded stunned.

Pike looked equally surprised and stroked his jaw while surveying his friend.

"What makes you ask that?"

"Am I right?" Quest countered Smoak's inquiry.

Smoak shrugged, his expression was confirmation enough.

"It's what your dad said about bringing all this down. Hill said almost the same thing when he came to see me at Mick's place in Chicago. Now I've just discovered that the very weapons I'm scraping from the division at Ramsey, Hill's buyin' 'em up as fast as I can sell them."

"Q-"

"Save it Pike," Quest raised a hand. "Just handle it. Get your family in order but just tell your brother to come to me for what he needs. I'll vouch for the discretion of my people, but there's no sense takin' any chances."

A Lover's Hate

"So are we done now?" Pike asked with a pleading grin softening his face. "I really hope we are 'cause I *really* need to find my wife."

"I damn well second that," Quest muttered.

Quay clapped Smoak's back. "You should go find my cousin. Tell her what you just told us."

Smoak's wince appeared more playful than pained. "She won't be nearly as easy to convince as y'all were."

Quay laughed. "Yeah...she is one hard ass...but think of what happens when she starts to trust in you again." He shrugged, "Makes it all worth it."

"Thanks man," Smoak shook hands with Quay again and watched him walk off. "That's what's keepin' me goin'," he told himself.

FIVE

"Jeez girl, did the guy catch all the moles or just the flattering ones?" Melina Ramsey queried as she observed the nude portrait of Sabra over the mantelpiece in the penthouse living room.

"*All* my moles are flattering, you hussy." Sabra drawled when she strolled over to take a closer look at her portrait. "You'll have to come to the bedroom to see the more revealing version." She said.

"You mean *that's* not it? Lord! The horror!" Bill ranted as if pained. She received a pillow thrown at her head for her trouble.

The reception had ended over a half hour earlier with the tossing of the bouquet; which Sybilla and Sabra refused to line up for. Alas, it was Carmen who emerged the lucky recipient of the toss.

Pike and Belle were separated by well-wishers then. The men ushered the anxious groom off for one last round of drinks in spite of his protests. Pike was more than ready

A Lover's Hate

to shut out the world for time alone with his wife. Sabra and Bill rounded up the bride, along with Mick, Ty, Mel, Johari and Nile. The ladies adjourned to Sabra's penthouse for drinks and to await their men.

"It really is exquisite work though Sabra." Melina had grown serious amidst her observation of the portrait. "Such detail," she noted while brushing her fingers across the artist's signature. "Does his color really well...these hues are right on point."

"Yeah...he was really talented." Melancholy crept over Sabra as she observed the piece. "You have to be sure to see the rest of his work around the resort before you leave." She told Melina.

"Are they sure it wasn't just an accident?" Michaela asked from her place cuddled into an oversized mauve armchair.

"Looks that way," Sabra left the painting and went to the picture window that spanned an entire wall. There waited an incomparable view that was the city of Las Vegas at night. She'd told her family what Smoak shared about Austin Chappell's death- the car running him over again and again.

"Did Smoak think you might know something about it?" Johari asked.

Sabra shook her head. "He just thought I should know." She looked away from the view but didn't turn completely around. "He didn't say there was any sort of link to me..." She knew Johari was remembering the loss of her own artist friend whose death was a definite link to Johari.

"Such a waste," Mel noted again, having turned from the painting. "Would've been great to have him out for a show," She referred to her place of business- Charm Galleries in Seattle, Washington.

"Speaking of shows," Mick tried to lighten the mood. "Do you really think our idea is solid?"

"Oh definitely," Mel sighed already switching gears at the mention of Mick's and Nile's idea to host an art show benefitting the young people Nile mentored in California. "Please be sure to thank the kids again for agreeing to part with the work for a while."

"Ah, they're happy to do it." Nile said, sliding down a bit on the sofa where she lounged. "They're so excited about the chance to attend an actual art gallery exhibition. I'll have the pieces shipped out as soon as I get to California. We're heading there right after we leave here."

Mick's attempt at changing the conversation succeeded. The women launched a discussion of the show details and what the proceeds would benefit.

Smoak arrived at the penthouse during the lively chatter. Sabra had an operator on standby to bring up the men in one of the express elevators. She left the penthouse lock unsecured so the guys could just walk in as they arrived.

Smoak was more than a little peeved over the fact that Sabra had been so careless but he realized that she was in her element. The last thing he wanted was for her to be unsettled there of all places. He decided he'd just have to do an impeccable job of watching out for her.

Smoak Tesano had polished the skill of watching a person so intently they couldn't help but feel the weight of his gaze. He could slip into a room unnoticed so easily, that the initial response to discovering him; quiet, dark as night and potently attractive, was oftentimes a reaction between distinct unease and utter fascination.

Such was the case when Sabra caught sight of him and gasped as much from his unexpected appearance as from the sheer appeal he exuded. The man was walking seduction or…coercion depending on who he was throwing his attention toward.

She couldn't look away as he relaxed against one side of the curved doorway leading into the living room. His movements were always unhurried, yet that barely masked the deft alertness residing just below the skin.

It didn't take long for the other women in the room to tune into their hostess' preoccupation. Soon, everyone was staring; with overt interest, at the riveting onyx-skinned male who had invited himself to their party.

Tykira and Sabella had been in the kitchen discussing their joys and anxieties about giving birth. They returned to the living room to break the spell Smoak had cast over the space. Happy to find him there, the women cried out his name in unison.

Ty was first to receive Smoak's hug and kiss to her cheek.

"Congratulations on the baby," he whispered into her ear as they hugged. "And thanks again for workin' so hard on this project." He gave her a playful frown. "Had I known you had all this goin' on," his eyes dropped to her waist, "I'd have reconsidered asking."

"Stop," Ty slapped his shoulder. "I've enjoyed working on this and we should talk before me and Quay head back."

"Tomorrow good?" Smoak asked.

Ty beamed. "Perfect." She got another hug and kiss and then ventured to the champagne colored settee near the window.

Next, Belle moved in for her hugs but she kept hold of Smoak's arm after they'd embraced. She handled the task of introducing her brother-in-law to those he may not have known. Conversation colored the room again as Smoak made new acquaintances.

And a new fan club, Sabra silently observed watching how subtly he charmed her cousins with his manner and intelligence. It was a talent that came as naturally to him as breathing when he deemed it fitting to use.

"Smoak, by any chance, did you notice whether our husbands were about to follow your fine example and make their way up here?"

Smoak grinned in response to Michaela's question. "They were um...*talking* about leaving when I was heading out."

"Shit," Melina hissed. "I'll probably pass out on my way back to the room."

Mick rolled her eyes and flopped back into her chair. "Got an extra set of PJs, Sabe?"

"Come on Mick, you know PJs and Vegas don't go together." Sabra teased, tugging one of Mick's curls on the way past her chair. She caught Smoak's eye briefly among the laughter that broke out and then she made a hasty escape to the quiet of her kitchen.

"Hey?" Sabella pulled Smoak to a quiet corner. "We'll text the guys and let 'em know to go on to the rooms instead of coming here." She squeezed his hands. "It's been a very long day, so we'll lock up while *you* say goodnight." She cast a saucy, suggestive look in the direction Sabra took to the kitchen.

"You're an angel," Smoak dipped his head to kiss Belle's cheek.

It took a minute or so before he spotted her. The kitchen was *that* expansive. It was state of the art and similar to what one might find in a small gourmet restaurant. He was; for a few seconds, preoccupied by thoughts of letting loose in there and cooking until his heart was content.

The easiness left his eyes then to make way for the shadow of concern when he saw her near an industrial sized chrome refrigerator. She had her back to him and her head was down while she braced her hands along the edge of the chrome counter space that almost ran the length of the wall.

Just then, a foreboding sense of dread riddled through him. What if he couldn't make this right? He frowned then moved his head once from right to left in a slow shake of defiance. He was done being without her.

On silent steps, he made his way to her taking in the length of her thick, midnight mane that almost brushed the small of her back. He smiled; recalling that she'd never cut or relaxed it because her mother disapproved. For a woman who lived her life being no-nonsense and bad-assed, the truth of it was, Sabra Ramsey was a soft heart in a hard shell. Yes, he was so done being without her.

"Nice picture," he complimented when he stood less than three feet away from her.

Her shoulders squared, but she didn't turn. "I didn't sleep with him if that's what you're getting at."

"That's not what I was getting at, Sweet."

"Oh bullshit," she faced him then. The look on her plump, maple brown face was beyond agitated.

Still, Smoak was captivated by the lovely oval. Her toffee-toned stare was almond shaped and vibrant. Model quality cheekbones and a small nose accentuated a generous mouth that curved in the most erotic manner.

"I know what you think of me," she mumbled while brushing her way past him. "Slut? Ho? Those terms bring back any memories, Smoak?"

"I don't think that." His clear, rich voice echoed in the kitchen.

"Oh?" The word came out in an ill-humored laugh. "Since when?"

"For a long time," he maintained his distance, "especially since last year."

She blinked, understanding but then waved him off. "I don't have time for it."

He wouldn't let her walk away from him that time. When he took her arm, she seemed to wilt.

"We can't discuss this now," her voice hollowed. "I have a house full-"

"They left."

She struggled in earnest then to fend off his hold. "I don't want to talk about it."

He jerked her hard, making her cease her struggles. "Talk about what?"

Her gaze faltered, but Smoak refused her the out. He tilted his head, keeping his eyes aligned with hers.

"Talk about what?" He insisted.

"Don't-"

"About why you looked at me like you didn't know who I was that morning?"

A Lover's Hate

Sabra jerked free then and slapped him. "Son of a bitch! Dammit, I said I don't want to talk about it!"

"Alright," he kissed her then. The act was hard, punishing and relentless.

Sabra melted instantly and participated with thorough eagerness. She could feel him easing his hold and she renewed her struggles hoping he'd believe they were for real. He tightened his grip again, but she continued to struggle fiercely until he took both her wrists and pushed her arms behind her back.

Softly she moaned the word yes and kissed him then as though she was drugged on the taste, smell and feel of his lean steely frame against her. Desire for him had her feverish.

He broke the kiss to work his mouth down her throat, using ravenous strokes of his sculpted lips and seductive tongue. His hand flexed about her wrists and he drew her deeper into his body- closer to the wet kiss he plied to the tops of her breasts heaving past her bodice. He was kissing her again, pulling her up high and then setting her down to the cool chrome cooking island in the middle of the kitchen.

His tongue battled hers with such force; she had little choice than to lie flat on the island. Smoak released her wrists and she grabbed his hand, silently instructing him to manacle her wrists again. He needed no further direction and kept her hands trapped above her head.

Sabra gasped on the fringe of a climactic surge. Smoak used his free hand to tug aside a portion of the diagonally cut bodice. Sabra heard the faintest rip as the fine material gave beneath his insistent tugs. She bit her lip on the sensation roused by the sound. Cool air breezed

AlTonya Washington

across a nipple once one of her double D cups was freed from its confinement.

Smoak merely outlined the mound which bounced an enticing dance against his lips. Sabra was almost insane with wanting to beg him to take her into his mouth. She dared not offer any words of encouragement for fear that he'd find fault in her eagerness and stop.

Smoak was already calling on his hormones to cool however. He pressed his forehead to the valley between her breasts and inhaled as if to clear his mind.

Sabra turned her face away and fought to stifle her tears. He freed her hands and she made quick work of fixing her dress.

He rose up over her, but didn't fully straighten. Instead, he kept his fists planted on either side of her on the island. His head was bowed, but he didn't look her way as his breathing slowed.

"We're meeting with Ty tomorrow to discuss the construction. I'll call when we've got a time." With those words, he moved and walked out of the kitchen.

Sabra stayed where she was until she heard the front door open and close. She scrambled off the island, stumbling on the dress hem and her heels as she raced to the living room and out to the foyer. She set the chains and deadbolts. Kneeling before the locked door, she succumbed to a massive bout of shivers. She was chilled to the bone.

SIX

Seattle, Washington~ May 1988...

9 year old Sabra Ramsey woke to the sounds of her parent's voices- the sounds of her parent's angry *voices.*

That was nothing new. Only the anger usually happened after Felix Cade had been in town at least a week. The couple had squared off against each other in the kitchen. Georgia stood near the stove, Felix at the refrigerator.

"You haven't been in town a week and already talkin' about another baby. Why do men always think that's what a woman needs to make her feel better?" Georgia put her hands to her hips and glared a little more fiercely.

"Tell me, just when would you *have a turn at raising the thing? When you just* happen *to drop in from California?"*

A Lover's Hate

Felix ran both hands through his thick hair. "Why do you always have to make everything a fuckin' battle?" His handsome licorice-toned face contorted into a glower.

Georgia wasn't cowed by the wild look in his dark eyes. "Why in hell do you think I'd even want to try *for another kid? We were lucky to have Sabra after I lost the first one."*

Some of the anger cooled in Felix's gaze. "You really think we're lucky, G? I know I *am. You've given me a beautiful baby girl. But what about you, Georgie? Did you ever really feel lucky to have her or was she an inconvenience? A time conflict with your busy schedule?"*

"Fuck you." Her voice was as soft as her walnut brown gaze and she settled back near the stove. "What would you *know about time conflicts? You're out livin' it up in California, aren't you?"*

"And you're livin' it up here as well." Felix reminded her. "Don't act like the down-trodden single mom when you can afford to have nannies here round the clock for the girl. She probably didn't even know you were her mama 'til she was six!"

"You get out! Get the fuck out of my house before I send you back to California with your kid! Then let's see you talkin' about havin' another baby!"

Felix threw up his hands. "Tell Sabra I'll be back to say goodbye."

"Mmm hmm," Georgia sneered, tapping her foot impatiently as she watched him storm from the kitchen.

Sabra stayed hidden in the corner down the hall where she'd overheard the fight. Tears leaked from her eyes faster than she could smear them away.

***

"Damn man, don't you ever sleep?" Caiphus was rubbing morning drowsiness from his eyes when he opened the door to his brother.

"Where is he?" Smoak asked once he'd clapped Caiphus' cheek and mussed the short dark curls crowning his head.

Caiphus moved aside and Smoak roamed the living room/rec room. The area was complete with separate plasma screens for TV viewing and gaming. A massive bar occupied the wall adjoining the two rooms. It appeared well used.

Faint clatter beyond the rec room caught Smoak's ear and he followed the sounds out to the kitchen. There, he found Hill preparing what looked to be some sort of hangover remedy.

"That bad?" Smoak called out.

Hill's fierce deeply bronzed features softened as a grin fell in place for his younger brother. "Mornin', Kid." He crossed the distance to Smoak and pulled him into a bear hug.

Smoak cherished the embrace, squeezing his eyes shut and then kissing Hill's cheek. "What the hell are you doin' here?" He asked.

"Chump takin' the vows is cause for celebration. If we could all be so lucky, huh?" Hill went back to the counter and poured another of the hangover concoctions. He passed the glass to Smoak and they clinked glasses in toast.

Smoak downed half the drink and then nodded toward Caiphus who had just stepped into the kitchen. "You fill him in?"

"Yeah," Caiphus was headed for the refrigerator.

A Lover's Hate

Smoak's gaze narrowed in obvious surprise.

"What?" Hill queried, having noticed his brother's expression.

Smoak set aside the glass and then leaned against the counter. "Just impressed is all." He surveyed Hill closely. "Thought you would've gone off wild and ravin' over what Dad told us."

Hill only shrugged and downed more of the drink he'd blended.

Smoak's ebony stare shifted to Caiphus' turquoise one with a knowing intensity. "You didn't tell him." It wasn't a question.

Hill was on alert then. His expression warned that clarification had better be forthcoming and quick.

Caiphus had poured juice instead of taking part in the hangover recipe. "I wasn't doin' that without backup." He sipped the OJ calmly.

Hill slammed down his glass.

Smoak didn't look away from Caiphus as he addressed Hill. "Dad finally confirmed what we suspected. He told us Gabe put Mama in that chair. He was getting too close to whatever this shit is and they went after him. Got her instead."

"Son of a bitch," Hill's voice was every bit of a growl and he slammed his fist repeatedly to the marble counter space. He stood there half a minute, his massive frame literally shaking with rage. When he moved from the counter, Smoak was there to block his passage.

"We can't go after the jackass."

"Fuck that."

Caiphus was shaking his head. "We can't man. Dad said."

"He's right Hill." Smoak met his brother's bottomless gaze with his own. "He said he'd be very *disappointed* in us if we went over his head on this."

Hill blinked as if coming down off a fraction of the madness inside him. He understood the meaning of the threat as well as his brothers. "Hell," he slammed his fist to the counter again that time clipping the blender and sending the tomatoey mixture spilling into the sink.

The bell rang and Caiphus went to answer, happy to escape the tension. Pike was the last person he expected to find on the other side of the door.

"What the fuck, man?" Caiphus laughed while hugging his brother. "Why aren't you in bed... havin' fun?" He winked devilishly.

Pike's grin belied subtle frustration. "Wish I was. Bella got up early to have breakfast with Bill and Sabra. Sabra called- somethin' she needed to talk about."

Pike was making the announcement just as he walked into the kitchen. The news only served to aggravate Smoak's already raw mood. Gnawing his jaw, he went silent for a time. Meanwhile, Caiphus explained to Pike what they'd just told Hill.

"He's right, man. Dad's damn well entitled." Pike said.

Hill kept his back turned until he'd wiped a hand across his eyes and took a deep drag of air. "Anything else I need to know?"

"Quest wants you to stop sneakin' around and come to him for weapons. Asked how long we were gonna keep pretending we're all on the outs." Pike said.

The news boosted Hill right out of his foul attitude and he grinned. "Christ, he's a smart muthafucka." He shook his head. "So that's it?"

A Lover's Hate

"As far as the meeting goes."

Everyone looked to Smoak who proceeded to tell his brothers about a car accident that really wasn't an accident.

"This guy Austin Chappell- was apparently on his way to see me. What?" He asked, having noticed Hill's reaction to the man's name.

"How do you know he was coming to see you?" Caiphus asked.

Smoak folded his arms across the BOSS emblem emblazoned on his T-shirt. "Some of the locals from one of the gas stations in town remembered him. He was asking for directions to my lab."

Smoak continued the story, including the visit six months prior to the accident on the last day of Sabra's trip to Phoenix. He told his brothers about the strange woman. "It may or may not be connected but after Chappell and folks calling Sabra to rattle me, I didn't feel good leavin' anything to chance. Apparently he's done some work here at the resort for her so…"

"Are you sure his name was Austin Chappell?"

That time, both Smoak and Pike were thoroughly focused on their brother's reaction.

"Yeah, Austin Chappell," Smoak confirmed.

"What was it about the woman that got you curious?" Hill asked.

"Tall as hell, weird smile almost like a child except when she saw me. Then she looked vicious just like that." Smoak snapped his fingers. "Psychotic for sure," he slid a look to Pike.

Both men waited for Hill to add more to the discussion. Indeed, Hill's expression had taken on a haunted undercurrent.

"Hill?" Pike stepped closer.

Hill raised a hand for quiet. "Can we finish this later?"

"How much later?" Smoak asked. "Is this the last time we'll see you for another year or two?"

"Too close to be taken out of the game now. Too close..." Hill sounded as if he were speaking to himself.

"Too close to what?"

"Please guys," Hill warded off Smoak's question with those words and another raised hand. He began to fan out the wrinkled gray T-shirt he wore as if he were suddenly overheated.

Smoak and Pike knew some new fouler aspect had come into the situation. Something had their brother spooked and Hilliam Tesano never got spooked.

Smoak wasn't about to let the man off the hook so easily. "Whatever this shit is, it involves Sabra. That's why I'm here and if you know somethin' I damn well expect you to tell it and good luck tryin' to shake me. You know me Hill, I'll be on your ass until you do."

"I don't think this has anything to do with Sabra." Hill assured with a slow, encouraging smile. "My guess is the woman knew her connection to Chappell and was trying to find him through her."

"Why?" Pike frowned.

"Can't say."

"Hill-"

"I promise I'm not tryin' to weasel out of sharing info, Kid but this is something new and I'm not altogether sure what it's about yet. I'm just asking you to give me some time. I promise not to leave you hangin'." Threading fingers through the wavy sleek locks that almost grazed his

A Lover's Hate

broad shoulders, he bowed his head and winced. "Please guys."

Again, Pike and Smoak let their gazes meet and then offered reluctant, simultaneous nods. Hill clapped their shoulders, pulled them close for a quick hug and then left the kitchen.

"Tell my cousins I'm on the way, I just need to take care of a few things before I get out of here…mmm hmm…"

Sabra was ending the call when Lee Lee walked into the private office.

"Sorry about last night, girl. I went to grab a change of clothes from my apartment and fell face down into sleep on my bed."

"It's alright," Sabra waved. "It was a draining day for everybody."

Lee Lee clasped her hands and smiled. "So were the bride and groom happy with the wedding?"

"Hmph," Sabra rolled her eyes. "I think they would've been happy with a justice of the peace. The wedding was a dream Lee-really. You did an excellent job." Sabra let Lee bask in the compliment for a while and then pointed a finger in her direction. "I'll hurt you if you're having any thoughts of quitting your job to become some kind of wedding planner."

"So um…how was last night?" Lee Lee asked once their laughter had quelled.

"I survived."

"Well," Lee Lee's eyes sparkled with promise. "Maybe you just overreacted-"

"Stop Lee, I won't argue over it again. I need you to do this."

AlTonya Washington

"And what about Smoak?"

Sabra began to straighten her desk. "What about him?"

"Do you still need me here since he's-"

"Nothing's changed there."

"Won't he have questions?"

"It'll be fine."

Lee Lee nodded, understanding that her friend would not be swayed. "I'll handle it first thing," she said.

"Wait a while," Sabra tugged at the drawstring bodice of the black lounger she wore. "I'm gonna take a shower first and then meet my cousins for breakfast."

Lee Lee turned and left the office. Sabra waited until she was alone to cover her face in her hands.

SEVEN

"Ms. Ramsey. Mrs. Tesano right this way."

Bill nudged Sabella as they walked arm in arm behind the host that escorted them into the restaurant were Sabra had arranged for a private brunch.

"That last name suits you." Bill noted to her cousin. "Don't even think about changing it again- it's got a nice ring to it."

"Ah well," Belle threw back her head and smiled. "You could have one just like it, you know?"

"Hmph," Sybilla smirked. "There a fifth Tesano son I don't know about?"

"Caiphus kept his gorgeous eyes on you almost the entire night."

"Jesus Belle, were you and Mama watching us the whole reception?"

"Not at all. We kept an eye on Smoak and Sabra too."

Bill laughed, but her smile thinned into a grim line all too soon. "I've been suspicious of him since I've known him." Her arms chilled under the capped sleeves of her rose blush blouse. "I don't know *how* to trust him," she confessed.

"Has he ever lied to you?"

"Belle!" Bill's whisper held an incredulous ring. "He tried to sabotage my job, remember? Had Lamont giving me all those bullshit assignments, told him we were sleeping together."

"But he didn't lie about it. He told you what he'd done."

"And that makes it alright?"

Belle's sigh was more like a lilt of faint laughter. "Maybe you could think less about *what* he did and more about *why* he did it."

Bill groaned. "You spend way too much time around my mother."

The host led them into the VIP dining room that had been closed especially for them. Brunch was on the menu but it was impossible to tell the time of day. The room was dim and elegant with a lifelike replica of the Vegas skyline at night.

The host had instructed them to begin and the women filled their plates in silence for a while.

"I had him checked out." Bill said, halfway through loading her plate.

"Oh?" Belle's voice was nonchalant as she pretended to focus on the elaborate spread.

"Caiphus supposedly leads some...*team* that Lamont apparently answers to. Can you believe that?" She chuckled halfheartedly. "Sounds like he and his crew can write their own ticket."

"Do you believe that?"

Bill shrugged. "I had it checked out…"

They took seats on a cushioned round black sofa that hugged a far wall.

"So," Belle kicked off the sandals she wore with a coral blouse and wrap skirt of the same color. "What are you gonna do?"

Bill picked at the fruit and cheese she'd loaded to her plate. "If I want in on this latest assignment, I may have to work with him. *For* him," She shuddered at the thought.

"Is that a shudder of excitement?" Belle bit into a strawberry to hide her smile.

"Try a shudder of dread."

"I don't believe you."

Bill leaned forward as if to share a secret. "Caiphus Tesano is not his brother- your husband."

Belle selected another strawberry. "And yet you love him anyway."

Sybilla nibbled her cheese and made no reply.

***

Seattle, Washington~ November 1989…

Swirls of fresh snow followed Georgia into her brother's spacious understatedly elegant home.

"West? Bri?" She called as she rushed in. She smiled at the sight of Briselle arriving in the long corridor leading toward the foyer.

"Did I miss dinner? Sorry I'm late." Georgia rolled her eyes, faking agitation. "Do Italians even celebrate Thanksgiving? I know some of 'em get sloppy drunk during it."

A Lover's Hate

"*Why are you drinking with Italians on Thanksgiving?*"

"*Are you serious?*" Georgia handed Bri her coat. "*The Tesanos? They've got another deal in the works with West. Christ, Bri don't you ever talk to your husband about what he does for a living?*"

Bri shrugged. "*Only when I'm having trouble sleeping,*" she hung the coat in the foyer closet.

Georgia rolled her eyes over the woman's apparent disinterest in things she herself found fascinating. "*I'm working up the PR for the latest endeavor. I was out with Gabriel Tesano.*"

"*And he just had to see you on Thanksgiving? Why?*"

"*It was business, Bri. Thanksgiving's a day like any other.*"

"*Hmph.*"

Georgia rolled her eyes over her sister-in-law's unimpressed response. "*You know Bri, not every woman spends her days ironing her husband's socks and jock shorts.*"

"*Now I take offence to that, Georgia. I do not iron West's socks.*"

Laughter roused between the women. Georgia hugged Bri tight. "*I'm starving. I went home, has Aiesha already brought Sabra over?*"

"*Well yeah she-*"

"*What about Damon and Catrina? Are they here yet with the boys?*"

"*Georgia,*" Briselle kept her sister-in-law from going further down the hall. "*Felix is here. He gave the sitter the day off and brought Sabra over, himself.*"

"I thought he wasn't coming 'til day after tomorrow?" Georgia's gaze shifted past Bri's shoulder and down the hall.

"Looks like he changed his mind."

Georgia heard the tension in Briselle's voice. "So what's he got his dick in a twist about now?"

"G."

Bri stifled her comment when Felix's voice sounded from a room down the hall. "We're all in back when you're done." She tried to sound encouraging.

Georgia watched Bri walk off. Then; with her head high, she went to the library where Felix waited.

"Close the door, G. Lock it," he added shortly.

She did as he asked and waited.

"Thanksgiving too, G?"

"Don't start." She went to fix herself a drink.

"Didn't you have enough of those with the Tesano?" He noted when she poured two fingers of Scotch.

"Eavesdropping on my conversations now?" She laughed.

"Sabi's sitter tells me the same thing every time I've called over the last two weeks. How old's that girl anyway? Sounds like a kid."

"Don't worry, she's legal. I wouldn't just have anybody watching our child, Felix."

"Right," Felix seemed unconvinced. "So, a meeting with Mr. Tesano. Gabriel, right? Don't bother confirming. That one's been tryin' to get between your legs since he met you."

Drink in hand, Georgia sauntered closer to Felix. The sequins on her red blouse sparkled as vibrantly as the anger in her glare. "And how many women literally push their numbers inside your pants? I've seen it, Felix."

A Lover's Hate

"I'm not the one with a ten year old girl at home."

"No you're not, are you?"

"Maybe you don't need to have a ten year old girl at home."

The quiet threat stopped Georgia. In all their years as parents, through all the arguments, Felix had never even hinted at taking Sabra from her. She went rigid from fury...and fear.

"So...finally ready to play daddy, huh?" She drew strength from her anger.

Felix remained cool. "I've always been ready." One hand disappeared inside a black trouser pocket while he used the other to point in her direction. "I've stood by all these years and waited for you to do the right thing by our girl and you've hardly raised her."

"Please! You will not come in here and put down the way I mother my daughter!"

"Our daughter! Jesus, you wouldn't even let her keep my last name!"

"You forget Felix, we were already divorced when she came along."

"And like a fool I let you get by with that shit."

"Thank you for admitting that you didn't make much of an argument about it."

"Maybe I'm making an argument about it now."

"You won't take her from me." Georgia spoke with quiet certainty lacing her words.

"Not even your last name could prevent that." Felix sounded just as certain. "Women don't just automatically get the kid so easy now, Georgie. Unlike you, who answer to your brother, I answer to no one. I've got plenty of time to give to my girl."

Georgia couldn't ignore the fear then as it slowly claimed dominance over the fury. Her heart started to beat in her ears and her hand trembled on the glass it clutched.

"You can't," she croaked.

"I promise you, I can."

"She's all I have, Felix."

"Spare the bullshit, G. I know you."

"Then look at me and tell me I'm lying."

"You don't even raise her."

"I swear that's exactly what I'm doing. I'm not trying to be a good little housewife like my mother was and Bri is. I love and respect them both very much but that's not the life I want. It's not the life I want for Sabra- letting the man take care of the bills while she takes care of the dishes." Georgia threw back some of her drink then. "She'll know hard work and sacrifice produces great success and the freedom to enjoy it."

"At what cost, Georgia? She's growin' up fast and you're not even around for it. Did you know the girl can read stock reports? I mean, she actually understands *the damn things? She's back there right now talkin' to West about why he should sell shares he's got in some gas company."*

Georgia looked pleased. "Of course I know. Who do you think taught her?"

Felix blinked, his attractive face was alight with surprise.

"I'm not just legs, big tits and ass Felix." She fixed him with a soft stare. "There really is a working brain in here. I love my girl and I'll fight anybody who says otherwise. I'll fight you *to hell and back if you try to take her from me. Now if you'll excuse me," she finished the*

Scotch and headed for the door, "it's not good to drink on an empty stomach."

***

Sabra stood near the row of black cabinets where she was locking up the Scotch she kept there. She caressed the label on the last bottle and wondered if she could handle a drink for old time's sake. She cursed inside her head and told herself she was thinking crazy.

Smoak's mere presence was bringing up all that old baggage. Sabra put up the bottle, closed the door resolvedly and locked it. She bounced the key against her palm and decided to give it to Lee Lee later on.

She rested along the counter and thought. It wasn't simply Smoak's presence. Something had changed about him and it had everything to do with that night last year. She told herself she didn't want to know, that knowing would make it real again. If she ignored it, it'd go away.

The truth of it was, she *did* want to know. Maybe knowing-*wanting* to know would probably be the beginning of getting to the bottom of it all…then what? She still wouldn't have him.

Memories flashed of the night before and she closed her eyes. She swayed in place over the way he felt, the way his hands…

"Stop it!"

"Huh?" Lee Lee was returning to the office and had overheard Sabra. "You still haven't showered?"

"Oh," Sabra glanced at the lounger she still wore, "um…no-got sidetracked and then Cheryl called about that damn hair show." She went back to her desk. "I don't know why she thinks I'm interested in that crap."

"Hmph, because you are."

Sabra couldn't help but smile. "Hell yeah," she admitted. Hair shows drew big crowds which made her big money. "But Cher wants me to be *in* the damn thing, Lee."

"And?" Lee Lee put a tired look in place. "Hell, if anyone can tame that wildness on top of your head it's Cheryl. I know *I'd* pay to see it."

"Screw you, Lee." Sabra patted the thick messy ball she'd drawn her hair into. "Anyway, we should schedule a meeting to discuss preliminaries."

Lee Lee was reaching for her e-tablet when her mouth fell open and she stared as if mesmerized.

"I got an appointment with Cheryl in a few days," Sabra was saying while she shuffled through papers in one of the desk drawers, "it'd probably be best to set the meeting before or after I get my hair done, you know? Lee Lee? Lee?" Sabra finally pulled her head out of the drawer and saw what had Lee Lee dumbfounded.

Smoak nodded toward the women. "Sorry for just walking in. Door was open." The look he slid to Sabra relayed his displeasure over the fact. Turning his attention back to Lee Lee, he smiled.

"Good to see you again, Lee."

"Yeah," Lee Lee nodded, slow at first, still mesmerized and then she gradually quickened the pace of her nods as she came to. "Good to see you Smoak. I understand we're to be doing some work with you."

"Hope to have some buildings constructed."

Sabra slammed the drawer shut and stalked out from behind the desk.

"I know how busy you are," Smoak continued to address Lee Lee, "but I'd appreciate a meeting sometime this week."

"Will you be leaving soon?" Lee asked.

"Not until my business is done." He smiled when Sabra's heavy sigh filled the air.

"Well I'll get a meeting down A-S-A-P." She went to the desk but turned just as she passed behind Smoak. Standing where only Sabra could see her, Lee Lee opened her mouth wide in a display of utter approval for the man in the room.

"I'll um, take care of that other matter later." Lee Lee collected herself and gathered her things. "I'll just give you guys some time alone."

"See you got an elevator key," Sabra noted when she was alone with Smoak.

"Lee was nice enough to include one to this tower."

"She's just so thoughtful."

"Isn't she though?"

"Look Smoak, I don't have time." Sabra briefly massaged her fingers to her temples. "I'm on the way to meet my cousins and I'm already mad late."

He shrugged beneath the crisp, dark shirt he'd changed into. "So what's a few more minutes?"

"A lot. I'm not in the mood to talk."

"Well then, we make a fine pair." Smoak didn't seem agitated by her unwillingness to cooperate. "I'm not in the mood to talk either."

At the determination in his gaze and stride, Sabra subconsciously retreated. Smoak caught her before her back hit the wall. Her fists curled at his chest, but Sabra didn't think to fight- or *pretend* to fight. That is, until she felt the wall at her back. She bristled and her lashes fluttered. Her lids closed over her eyes when his mouth worked its way from her earlobe to her collarbone. Attempting resistance then, Sabra flattened her hands against his shoulders and pressed.

AlTonya Washington

"Stop fighting me," he gave her a hard warning jerk.

She wouldn't listen and continued to 'resist' until he lost patience, captured her wrists and held them above her head to the wall. His mouth worked across her collarbone while his free hand lifted the flowing hem of her gown.

"Stop fighting me," his rich voice was muffled into her skin.

The faint graze of his hand across her thighs, sent Sabra's legs parting and promising to give way when his fingers disappeared inside her. They lingered for only a few seconds. Smoak used his thumb to stimulate her clit and she whimpered as her head drifted to his shoulder. Struggling to inhale, her whimpers turned to ragged moans.

"What is this damn thing you're wearing?" Collaring her neck in his hand, he feasted on her earlobe. "Get out of it," he murmured. "Do it," he ordered when she didn't move fast enough.

Hands shaking as much as the rest of her, Sabra tugged the drawstring ties at the bodice. The sound of the material shifting mingled with the comforting hum of the air-conditioning. As she tugged down the material covering her body, Smoak's mouth seared every newly exposed inch of her maple skin.

A wavery moan slipped past her throat when he switched his preference from earlobe to nipple. In one fluid move, he had her free of the material swaddling her feet.

Sabra loosely draped her shapely legs about his lean hips and curved her nails into the sleek hair at the back of his neck. She reveled in the way he handled her, cradling her ass in his wide palms while he carried her through the apartment.

A Lover's Hate

Magnificent waves of arousal coursed through Sabra as his fingertips stroked the hypersensitive cavern between her buttocks. Somehow, his thumb continued its assault on her clit. Then it was *her* turn to nibble *his* earlobe. The cologne on his skin was an added stimulus.

"Smoak?"

"Mmm…?"

"Make sure the door's locked."

"*Now* she cares…"

EIGHT

Smoak's every intention was to carry his dark lovely burden to the first bed he found. He cleared the corridor adjoining the office and apartment, and then settled for the first chair inside the bedroom. His dick had extended long and painfully hard against his thigh. Until he was inside her, he couldn't think. Sabra's small moans; as she suckled his ear and nudged her nipples against his had him wild with wanting her. Wilder than he usually was, that is.

Living in Phoenix, while she was in Vegas, took the edge off but barely. The women he'd taken to his bed over the years had been poor substitutes for the one in his arms then, rubbing her sex across his and whimpering over the way it affected her.

It wasn't their fault. Other women were of little use to him save the obvious. He wanted everything Sabra had to give him- or simply had to give. He'd convince her of that one way or another, but later. Later...

He cradled her ass again once he'd freed himself. Then, he settled her suddenly. Sabra gasped into his shirt and bit into the sinews of his shoulder when he filled her. That stiffness so longed for, so missed...it was like having a craving satisfied after so long.

He didn't wait for her to adjust to his size; given her tightness which he must have felt.

"Jesus Sabra..." he let his head fall back to the chair. His palms were greedy for her, squeezing and lifting her bottom. He maneuvered her up and down his shaft so that she rode him to his satisfaction.

Sabra locked her hands over the arms of the chair and angled her hips clockwise and counter. Her hair slipped from the weak confines of the messy chignon and; in moments, her thick locks fell in a tousle about her lush, beautiful face. Her mouth formed a perfect O, yet no sound emerged. Her breasts bounced before his face, nudging the chiseled curve of his jaw. Gradually, sound passed her lips as she added speed to her ride.

"Slow down," Smoak tapped her bottom once.

Sabra obeyed. The order was as orgasm inducing as the rod of onyx steel inside her. She reached up to pull away the band that had been binding her hair. Just then, the simple bow only hung on by a few tendrils. Sabra lost her fingers in the thick mass and once again added speed to the rotations of her hips.

"Fuck..." Smoak slapped her derriere with both hands that time. "Slow down dammit...makin' me come..." his head fell back to the chair again.

Sabra refused to obey on purpose. She punched the granite wall of his chest that was visible thanks to her maneuverings which had loosened the buttons along his shirt.

Smoak tapped her bottom again and gave a warning squeeze. Sabra punched him again, biting her lip on a smile when he grabbed her hands and shackled her wrists at the small of her back.

"Mmm...yes..." she breathed, elated and she slowed her bounce up and down the carefully crafted beauty of his wide shaft.

He cupped her breast, sliding the nipple down his cheek, beneath his nostrils and across his lips before taking it inside his mouth and just barely sliding his tongue across the marble surface that pouted for his attention. Smoak grunted then, filling his mouth with one of the full sweet mounds. She drenched him as she peaked and he could feel her heart beating through her breast in his mouth.

She wanted to melt when he came. His warmth filled her like a gooey treat. She'd literally dreamed of him this way. He'd denied her for so long, to finally have him seemed like another dream. She wouldn't think of what came next or what he'd demand for the wisp of heaven he was granting her.

She flexed inner walls about him and coaxed every drop of moisture from the tip of his sex. Smoak was still suckling her nipple ravenously. He stopped to hide his dark face between her breasts and subjected her nipples to dual thumb massages while his tongue bathed the satin skin of the fragrant valley.

Long after their climaxes were spent, they cuddled on the chair, bodies still lustfully connected. Sabra kept her eyes squeezed shut. She wasn't ready for reality to set in.

Smoak wasn't ready either. He hadn't thought about the consequences of coming there and doing what they'd done. Would it relax her enough to be honest with him about that night? He doubted it. It would take much more to persuade her to trust him.

Much more of this? He wondered, weighing the plush fullness of her bottom. God, he hoped so.

***

Sabra showered and changed once Smoak left. They didn't make love again. Make love? Is that what they'd done? Had they ever done that? Sex between them had never been tender or gentle- delicate… It had been tumultuous, intense, uninhibited. But she was changed now. Their last time together…it changed her.

There was another element now. Whether it was newly added or merely recovered after years of suppression, she didn't know. How could she share that with him and not have him believing she was the slut he'd once labeled her? She'd definitely deserve that label then, wouldn't she? Anyone would think so.

Quick knocking and the click of the front door lock caught her ear. She was curled on the soot-gray sectional sofa in the living room. There she waited, dressed in a fresh white linen lounger and armed with a mug of aromatic Peppermint tea. She winced apologetically when her cousins rounded the doorway into the room.

"Lee Lee gave us the key," Belle waved the card once before dropping it to a small round table near the door.

"She also told us Smoak was here." Bill added.

"Sorry y'all."

"Don't worry about it." Bill strolled toward the sofa, her gait lazy but her gray stare alert as she surveyed. Once she'd drawn near to Sabra, she leaned in slightly and let her nostrils flare. "Washed your hair," she said, "things got sweaty, huh?"

"Don't," Sabra shuddered and folded her hands tighter about the warm mug.

"Well why don't *you* start?" Belle encouraged while settling to one of the deep chairs facing the sofa. "We're pretty sure you didn't arrange brunch just so we could have girl time together."

Sabra sipped at her tea and prayed the hot minty liquid would go to work calming her. "This isn't easy to talk about," she spoke into the mug. "I um…I've never told anyone. Lee Lee doesn't even know all of it."

Belle shot a quick look toward Bill and then left the chair to sit closer to Sabra on the sofa. "Would you rather talk to Smoak?"

"Hmph," Sabra curled into a tighter ball. "*That* is the problem. This isn't something you just walk up and share-especially with a man."

"Honey you're starting to scare us." Bill said from her perch along the back of the sofa.

"I'm sorry."

"Stop doin' that," Bill snapped, "just tell us what the hell is goin' on with you. Lee says you've been actin' like some sort of crazy woman since Smoak took over those floors in the other tower."

Sabra left the sofa and walked barefoot to the wall holding her portrait. Behind her, Belle and Sybilla exchanged another round of stares.

Bill cleared her throat and slid down from the back of the sofa to claim the spot Sabra had just abandoned. "Remember how sick I was growin' up?" She waited for Sabra to turn. "It's not easy to tell anybody that you've lost control of your bowels in bed…" She swallowed on the memory. "But when I told you guys that, I knew my secret would always be safe."

"Thanks girl," Sabra's voice was a shudder but she did smile. "We never made it to the bed, just the chair-"

Sabella began clapping gleefully at the news.

"It was just to work off frustration, Belle. Nothing was settled."

"Ha! I think Smoak would disagree with that." Bill mused, her small face alive with laughter.

Sabra set the mug to an end table and sighed. "He left almost right after we finished."

"Honey what is it you think you can't tell him?" Belle asked.

"You guys remember what happened in college after I...slept with Brogue?"

"You made a mistake."

"Bill..." Sabra shook her head. "That's how *we* see it. Men never see it that way. If you two weren't my cousins, you'd be callin' me a slut to the highest power. Don't lie." She said, just as Sybilla opened her mouth to argue.

"Sabi, what's this about?" Belle asked.

"It's about me performing the trifecta of betrayals. Sleeping with another man-" she raised her thumb, "his cousin-" she raised her index finger, "his *white* cousin." Her middle finger extended. "How could he forgive that? You know men don't get past that shit the way women do or pretend to."

"Sabi-"

"No Belle," Sabra waved, "this isn't even all about that. That's just where it started. When he told me I could go that day, he called me a slut but it wasn't just because

I'd slept with Brogue. He said he practically raped me and I moaned the whole time. He was right, I did."

The other women in the room were silent.

"I liked it. What he did- the way he did it. Everything." She spread her hands out to her still-silent cousins. "Anymore advice? I didn't think so," she said when they remained quiet.

"Have you...talked to anyone?"

Sabra's smile was sad. "So quick to label me a psycho, Bill?"

"Oh! Honey I didn't mean-"

"You're right. I should've talked to someone a long time ago, but I didn't." Sabra pulled all ten fingers through her hair. "Besides, it wouldn't do well for it to get out that the owner of one of Vegas' biggest and baddest resorts is a submissive. I don't care if it *is* Sin City, I doubt my rep would survive some shit like that."

"Baby your first responsibility is to yourself." Belle's chestnut brown stare was focused and steely. "How long do you think you can run a business with this driving you crazy?"

"What if I can't be fixed Belle?" Sabra's voice held a childlike echo. "What if I'm stuck like this for the rest of my life?"

"Did you enjoy your time with Smoak this morning?"

Bill's sudden question, brought weakness to Sabra's legs. She settled to an armchair. "Yes," she almost moaned the word.

"Well whether you tell anyone else or not is secondary. You at least need to tell *him*."

Sabra shook her head at Bill. "You're crazy."

"He's still the man you love, isn't he?"

A Lover's Hate

"That's not the point." Sabra continued to shake her head.

"That's exactly the point." Belle countered. "In the bedroom. In bed with the man you love is the place for total surrender- mind and body and on both sides."

"He's already called me the worst things and on several occasions." Sabra's gaze blurred with tears. "I'm not really eager to hear them again. If he knew this-"

"What makes you think he doesn't already know?" Bill tucked her feet beneath her on the sofa and leaned forward. "Sabra the man designs weapons for a living. His IQ is at genius level and while you may be-*may* be a submissive in the bedroom, you're not one in life. If you were, we wouldn't be sitting in one of *two* scrapers that carry your name and are the envy of almost every casino owner on this strip."

"Bill's right, Sabi. Chances are, you've already given him clues about your wants, your desires when the two of you are close."

"It's not fair for you to keep this hidden. He should share the burden of knowing. After all, it was his fault this happened. All this started after that day, right?"

But it's not his fault. Sabra kept her thoughts silent but Bill's words sent a pain through her heart. She couldn't let Smoak think this was his fault. If somehow he figured it out, he would surely think so.

Belle left the sofa and came over to kneel before Sabra. "Talk to him, honey. Soon. What do you have to lose?" She looked back at Sybilla and they both nodded, deciding they'd given their cousin even more to consider.

Belle kissed the top of Sabra's head and Bill followed suit.

AlTonya Washington

"I can't tell him," Sabra spoke to the room once her cousins were gone. It had been like hell telling everything to Belle and Sybilla.

But that's not true, is it? She acknowledged. There were secrets even those closest to her didn't know. She shook away that train of thought and returned to the matter at hand. Bill was right. Smoak was too smart not to start questioning the 'indications' she'd been making, especially if they had sex again. While her new...predilection hadn't reared its ugly head until after their explosive afternoon together, the seeds had been planted long before.

And just how was she supposed to get him to believe he wasn't at fault if she didn't tell him how she believed the whole thing got started.

She screamed then, taking fistfuls of hair and pulling tight at her scalp. She had to get out of there before she ran herself crazier.

When in doubt, she thought, work.

NINE

Smoak was quite obviously surprised by the sight greeting him when he arrived at a bistro in the lobby of the tower where he'd claimed residence.

Pitch Tesano presided over a large round table in the center of the lightly occupied dining room. It was a good thing too, since it seemed all the waitresses were interested in seeing to the man's every whim.

"Hey! Hey!" Pitch saw Smoak and bellowed a laugh as he clapped. "What's my nephew drinkin'?!"

If the waitresses had gone ga-ga over Pitch's copper kissed features, they were literally awe struck by Smoak's intense appeal.

"Bourbon for my nephew."

"And will you be needing anything else?" A waitress inquired of Smoak. Her light eyes confirmed the fact that she definitely meant 'anything'.

A Lover's Hate

Another waitress pressed a menu to his chest before he could reply. The leather bound portfolio was the only thing between Smoak and the woman's barely concealed bust.

"Thank you," his smile was politely cool and he nodded once. "I think I've got everything I need just now."

The waitresses eventually gave the men their privacy. Smoak set the menu down and then rounded the table to join his uncle in one of the smothering bear hugs Pitch Tesano had perfected.

"First chance we've had to talk." The man planted a hard kiss to his nephew's cheek. "How you doin, Kid?"

Smoak didn't conceal the faint traces of a scowl. "Definitely been better."

"Bah!" Annoyance triggered the gruff sound. "You need to go get that curvy beauty of yours and take her to bed. That'll fix you up in a heartbeat. Take my word!"

Pitch's gregarious laughter was highly contagious and Smoak was quickly joining in.

"I've already done that and it helped more than you know." Smoak pushed away from his uncle. "Things are still a mess though."

"Right…" Pitch stroked his collarbone visible past the neckline of a silk olive green shirt. "It's not so easy when you love 'em is it?"

Sadness belied Smoak's grin. "No Sir…no Sir, it's not."

"Sorry Kid… guess your Dad's meeting didn't help matters much either."

"Hmph," Smoak eased a hand into his back jean pocket and clenched the other into a fist against his thigh. "It's like tryin' to make a word with no vowels."

AlTonya Washington

Pitch chuckled. "Good example. These pieces are all over the place, aren't they?"

"What do you think's going on, really?"

Pitch reached for his drink and sipped while contemplating the question. A waitress returned with Smoak's drink and Pitch's dark gaze crinkled with appreciation.

"Thanks," Smoak took the drink and waited for his uncle to cease his survey of the busty Latina. Smoak observed the man closely and; for the first time, noticed how much he looked his age then. Smoak could see his facial muscles settling into familiar lines of a haggard expression. He knew Pitch had spent much time mulling over what may or may not have been going on in the Tesano family.

"Whatever it is, it's something insidious."

Smoak set aside the drink without tasting it. His dark eyes sparkled raptly as he waited for Pitch's next words.

"You've got no idea what it was like growing up with those three," his expression held a haunted element.

Smoak managed a weary smirk. "I think you know I do." He saw recollection come to Pitch's face.

Over the years, uncle and nephew had developed a bond that came from a place of mutual understanding. Smoak had always had the love and security of his immediate family. It was the bond with Pitch however that had made the uglier aspects of his childhood bearable.

"And they called *me* a bastard." Pitch glared into his drink before swallowing it down. "Thank God for Aaron," he smiled at the thought of his older brother.

Smoak reclined in a cherry wood Chippendale chair. "Is there more to his being sick than we were told?"

A Lover's Hate

"Doesn't seem to be," Pitch shrugged. "Ari's a tough mutha."

The men raised their glasses in silent toast to the second Tesano brother. When their glasses lowered, so did their moods.

"So what is it you, dad and the others hope we'll find?"

"A way to shut this shit down," Pitch said simply. "Me, Rome and Ari got out a long time ago. Vale is next in line to take over Papa's business. Your dad was right, Smoak. Gabe and Humphrey taught him well. He's worse than the two of them ever were and ready to continue whatever sickness they were involved in."

Smoak studied a wall painting that hung over a white baby grand piano across the bistro. "What about Brogue? How does *he* fit into all this?"

"Brogue…" Pitch massaged the area between his heavy brows. "He's the wildcard in all this."

"Wildcard?" Smoak almost laughed. "We've pretty much known where he's stood since childhood- with his dad." His eyes narrowed toward his uncle. "You can still call him that after everything he's pulled?"

"There's somethin' goin' on with that boy I can't put a finger on."

Smoak propped his elbows to the table. "Are you saying you think his loyalties have changed?"

"I wouldn't go *that* far. Maybe not changed so much as…matured."

Smoak's laughter rang out full-bodied and infectious across the semi crowded room. "Now *that's* even harder to believe."

"Stranger things have happened, young man." Pitch grinned, equally amused.

Smoak couldn't help but consider all that had happened over the very short span of time that he'd been in Vegas...with Sabra. Again, he raised his glass toward his uncle. "You've definitely got a point," he said.

***

"Well I should be back in a few days; things are still a little heated on this end. You know how it is when family gets together."

Pamma Nelson chuckled over her boss's words. "Say no more. But I do want to hear all about the wedding when you get back."

"Definitely," Sybilla switched her cell to her left hand and dug for the wallet in her bag. "I can tell you it was very beautiful. Every woman should be so lucky." Extracting the tan leather wallet, she pulled out a few bills for a tip. "I won't even get started on the reception," she told her assistant.

"Sounds like a story there," Pamma noted.

"You've got no idea," Bill sighed, wiggling sandal shod feet that didn't quite reach the carpet beneath them.

"Well don't worry about us back here."

"Are the guys getting restless?" Bill referred to her team.

Again Pamma chuckled. "I think they're actually enjoying the downtime. They know how fast things can turn around."

"Yeah..." Bill's agreement curbed into silence when she spotted Caiphus with Westin and Damon in the lobby. "Pam I'll talk to you soon, okay?" She disconnected from the call before the woman replied. Dropping the tip to the table, she scooted off the chair and made her way from the lobby bar in the second tower of Sabra Ram's.

A Lover's Hate

Trekking across the rose-blush and cream checkered floor teeming with bodies, she caught up to the men as they rounded the corner to the elevator bay.

Westin was the first to see his daughter. His handsome dark features were soft with adoration.

Despite her suspicions, Sybilla's gray stare filtered with love at the sight of her father. The two of them shared a lengthy hug once she'd approached. Sybilla savored the hug from her uncle as well before turning to the man at Damon's left.

"Caiphus."

"We spent the morning on that golf course of Sabra's- thing's a monster." West explained, removing the blue cap he wore and wiping sweat from his brow.

"What was the name again?" Damon asked his brother.

"Sabra's Greens."

Everyone shared a hearty laugh over the woman's never ending vanity.

Sybilla surveyed Caiphus with a distinct chill in her uncommon gaze. "I didn't know you played."

"Whenever I have the time," Caiphus cast a lopsided grin toward Westin and Damon. "I should've probably stayed in bed this morning- these guys are a little too far out of my league."

The brothers obviously appreciated the flattery. Their laughter drew several complimentary stares.

"You should see this one in action." West shared the spotlight with his daughter. "She can damn well hold her own on a course."

"Is that right?" Caiphus shifted his extraordinary gaze in Sybilla's direction. "I'll have to get her out there sometime."

"So um, what are you guys about to get into?" She quickly asked her father and uncle, praying they didn't catch the underlying meaning of Caiphus' words.

West sighed. "Off to see our wives."

"And get our orders for the rest of the day." Damon added, sounding as though he were looking forward to it.

An elevator car arrived just then. A stocky operator tipped his cap and called for riders going up.

"Comin' man?" West clapped Caiphus' shoulder.

"I'll get the next one, Sir."

"Suit yourself," West caught Bill's wrist and effortlessly lifted her off her feet. "Gimme some sugar."

Caiphus bit his lip as he grinned at the scene. No one would take the woman; presently giggling like a small girl, for one of the top agents in her field.

Bill received more kisses from Damon and then waved the men off before bringing her focus back to Caiphus.

"Still kissing up to my dad, I see."

Caiphus wiped his sunglasses on the hem of the white Polo shirt he sported. "Your father and uncle are two of the coolest men I know. Besides," he finished with the glasses, "it's good for a guy to spend time with his future father-in-law."

Sybilla threw her head back to laugh and missed Caiphus' bright eyes following the flip and bounce of her unruly hair.

"Do you ever quit?" She asked.

Caiphus wasn't amused and suddenly moved forward until he'd successfully crowded her in a blind spot near the elevators.

"Not until you're wearing my ring, my last name and maybe not even then."

A Lover's Hate

Bill maintained her cool and played along, somehow ignoring her heart in her stomach. "I could never marry a man who didn't want me to work."

"I don't have a problem with that. In fact," he trailed the stem of his sunglasses across her jaw. "I've got all sorts of jobs in mind that you can do for me."

Bill only shook her head. Her ability to maintain her cool was fast evaporating.

"Have you made up your mind about the case yet?"

"I don't even know what the 'case' is," she watched him with renewed interest. "Lamont's being so tight lipped, he won't even tell me much more than I already know. It connects to my uncles and the whole Cufi Muhammad situation, but how?"

"You're accepting? Before you answer," he cautioned when her lips parted, "remember this means you'd be working for me." He trailed the glasses down her neck. "Think before you say yes to me. There's no going back after that."

She swallowed and raised her chin a tad. "You give this same speech to all your employees?"

"No. This one's special for you." His smile was smugness epitomized. "You want to know more? Give me your answer."

"That's blackmail."

"Blackmail?" He winced. "I prefer to think of it as persuasion."

"Coercion."

"Encouragement."

"Ah…" Bill rested her head back on the wall. "The thought of you as my boss is supposed to be encouraging?"

His expression more than hinted that he was all too interested in proving that to her. "You're hitting brick walls with your investigation, Bee. I can help you with that but I want to hear it from you, not Lamont. You want in, you'll have to swallow all that pride and tell me so."

Closing the very little distance resting between them, he propped her chin on his fist and brushed his mouth across hers. Then, he was gone.

***

Sabra deserted her pity party and dressed in a suit that shrieked her trademark sassy and seductive style. The three-tiered cotton dress boasted complimentary tones of olive, sandstone, charcoal and silver gray. The lowest tier stopped several inches above the knee while spiked-heeled olive toned booties accentuated the length and shapeliness of her legs.

A typical day for Sabra began with a meeting with her food and beverage manager Zion Bigelow. As Zion had already left on vacation with his wife, Sabra took the meeting with his assistant. Mid-morning saw a succession of similar meetings with other members of her extensive staff. She often skipped lunch or grabbed a sandwich while taking in dress rehearsals of the entertainers for the various stage events and club performances.

Sabra stood commending Lavender Webster, one of the choreographers for the many erotically charged shows the resort featured at one of its numerous night clubs. As Sabra Ram's was unofficially an adult's only establishment, the shows tipped the scales between R and X-rated and could be enjoyed around the clock.

Lavender had gone up on stage to give instruction to one of the dancers. While waiting for the man's return, Sabra danced in place, enjoying the beat of the song piping through the club's state of the art speakers.

A Lover's Hate

"I think it'd please your guests very much to see you on one of your stages."

Sabra froze and then turned.

"I know your male ones would be very appreciative." Brogue Tesano predicted.

"What are you doing here?" Sabra whispered after spending half a minute giving him the once over.

Brogue shrugged, his sea-blue stare glinting wickedly. "Can't a high roller drop in unexpectedly for a drink…hug from the owner?"

An easy smile came through for Sabra. Seconds later, she was enveloped in an embrace and getting a kiss to the neck as well.

"What are you doing here?" She asked again when he let her pull away just a tad. "Your family's all over the place."

"Yeah, I know," he locked his arms about her waist and sighed, "Guess I'll have to start having to make a point of calling you before I just drop in, huh?"

"That'd be a good idea. Smoak's here."

"Right," his eyes narrowed as a frown emerged between his brows. "That's good."

Frowning as well, Sabra felt Brogue's forehead with the back of her hand. "Is your bad timing a result of poor health?"

Grinning then, Brogue pulled her hand from his head and kissed it. "I've definitely been better," he studied her hand in his, "and I know I'm risking having my face smashed in but I'm still sane enough to know what I'm doing."

Sabra tugged at the open collar of his black denim shirt. "Would you mind sharing it with me, then?"

AlTonya Washington

"Later. *This* isn't the best place for talking." He glanced past her shoulder. "All I keep thinking about is seeing you up there on that damn stage." He pulled her into another hug when she slapped his arm.

Sabra knew Brogue well enough to know when he was on edge about something. Given that he was the one who most often set others on edge, the situation had to be very serious to affect him the way she sensed.

"Can you at least give me a hint? You're concerning me." She admitted.

"Don't worry," he tugged away a curl that had been clinging to her cheek. "I'm not on the job," he gave her a wink that succeeded in making her laugh.

"I miss that sound," he said. "I'm sorry I ever gave you a reason to stop using it."

"Brogue you-"

"Stop," he shook his head. "You know what I mean. Sabra whatever you come to learn about me, just know I consider you a real friend. Maybe the only one I've ever had."

"Brogue-"

"What I did that night I- I took advantage of the situation."

"I threw myself at you," she argued, "I know I did that." *I must have*, she tacked on silently.

His light eyes raked her body as if to size her up. "I could've stopped you easy enough," he decided in a playful tone and then shook his head. "I knew you weren't yourself that night."

Sabra gasped.

"And we'll take it from the top again people! Sabra check this out!"

A Lover's Hate

Sabra turned to wave at Lavender's request. When she looked back for Brogue, he was gone.

TEN

"Nat!"

Late afternoon found Sabra back in her office and yelling out to Lee Lee's assistant Natalie Getty.

"Where the hell is Lee?! I can't get her on any line!"

Instead of yelling, Natalie used her phone and selected the speaker setting for Sabra's office. "She said she'd be back late from lunch- had something to take care of. She sounded very secretive about it."

"Oh," Sabra perched on the edge of her desk and faced her phone. "Was it something inside the resort?"

Natalie didn't answer and Sabra could feel her heart lurching in anticipation of the response. "Nat?" She could hear the young woman's faint laughter on the other end of the line.

A Lover's Hate

"Jesus," Sabra pushed off the desk to investigate. When she arrived from her office she saw what or *who* had Natalie in such high spirits.

"Got a minute?" Smoak asked when he saw her.

Nodding curtly after she stood gawking at him for ten seconds, Sabra smoothed her hands across her hips and then led the way back to her office. She ordered her feet to keep moving while periodically squeezing her eyes shut to rid her mind of the images of them together earlier that day. Inside her office, she successfully summoned a cool demeanor and waited for him to begin the discussion.

"I won't apologize for this morning." He said.

His words made her smile. "Guess your vow not to touch me is out the window."

His smirking triggered the dent in his cheek. "I was an idiot to think I could do that." He rubbed his abs, concealed behind the coffee brown shirt hanging outside his jeans, and then he closed the space between them.

"I know what happened doesn't change anything."

"Why should it?" Sabra gave a quick toss of her head. "It was only sex."

"You believe that?" He moved in closer.

"Don't you?"

"Do you think I'd have come here from Phoenix if I did?"

Sabra rolled her eyes then. "I don't know what to think," she sighed as though the admission relieved some weight. Curls tapped her back rhythmically as she began to walk the room. "I feel like I'm about to lose my mind and you and your cousin aren't helping any."

"My cousin?"

The clear depth of his voice seemed to send the words vibrating through her. "Brogue's here," she said while turning. She gave him a resolute smile. "In the resort. Has a suite. I don't expect you to believe I haven't visited him there. But he does stay here quite frequently." She saw no need to hide the fact. *Let him rage over it,* she thought. Maybe he'd become furious enough to leave and her life could get back to normal.

Smoak maintained his silence. His deep, dark eyes provided no clues to his mood at all.

"He's one of my high rollers," she went on, "he and his friends make me lots of money since most of 'em can't gamble worth a damn." Sabra realized she was rambling but she didn't see the need to stop at that point. "He had no idea the wedding was this weekend so…it was just poor timing on everyone's part."

Smoak tilted his head up, then down for a simple nod. "That's good."

"What?" She moved closer, feeling the stunned affect claim her once more that day. When he smiled, her heart flipped. "Are you alright?" She asked to dismiss the emotion the gesture stirred.

"I need to talk to him."

She blinked, trying to read beyond his words, but failing. "Okay…" she threw up her hands. "Well I've got stuff to do."

He caught her arm before she could get past him. "I need to talk to you too."

Her breath expelled as a shudder when she bowed her head. "Does it even matter to you that this terrifies me?"

Her admission sent relief surging through him then. Soon he was mimicking her actions and bowing his head as well. Tugging her arm, he held her tight to him.

"Talk to me," he spoke the words against her temple.

"It's easier for you to go on hating me." Her voice was hollow, lost.

"And you could live with that? Because *I* couldn't."

Noise from the hallway pulled them apart before Sabra could voice a response. Lee Lee was already speaking, even before she cleared the doorway.

"Alright, I've got everything back in place on-"

"Smoak's here." Sabra quickly made the announcement.

"Oh! Uh, hey," Lee Lee's smile reflected the same awe and surprise it'd held when she saw Smoak earlier that day.

"Lee Lee, I actually stopped in to see about setting that meeting with Ty. Tomorrow's their last day in Vegas." Smoak referred to Tykira and Quaysar. "She already talked to her crew. They'll be in from Colorado before lunch."

"Well let's see here…" Lee Lee was all business then as she sat to open her planner and look through Sabra's day.

While Lee perused the schedule; murmuring to herself about issues that were pressing and ones that could be changed, Smoak kept his eyes locked on Sabra's. He dared her to be the first to look away which she was. Silently, she was cursing herself over what she'd revealed before they were interrupted.

"Alright, so if we can do something around one-thirty, that'd be great."

AlTonya Washington

Smoak kept his eyes on Sabra for a few additional seconds before shifting it toward Lee Lee. "Sounds good. We could make it a lunch meeting."

"Perfect," Lee left the sofa, making her way for the office door. "I'll get started on the preparations."

"Lee! Um..." Sabra trailed off, her expression relaying to Lee Lee that she should stay. "So I'll see you tomorrow Smoak?" Smoothly, she suggested an end to their conversation knowing it would resume once Lee Lee was gone.

"We should really take a look at the land." He'd read her motives easily.

Sabra's frown reflected curiosity and agitation. "I look at the land every day."

"And when was the last time you looked at the undeveloped part of it?"

She had no rebuttal.

"We'll take a walk around the grounds. Pick you up at seven-thirty." Casually, he backed toward the door. "It'll still be hot as hell but the sun won't fry us quite as much." His bottomless gaze roamed her body leisurely and with unmistakable delight. "Dress appropriately." He advised before he left.

***

Monterey, California~

Carmen Ramsey left Las Vegas the previous day once the wedding reception drew to an end. Her family had begged her to stay on and enjoy the town for a few more days, but she declined. There were other things she wanted to enjoy.

"What?" She asked, feeling Jasper Stone's big body shake beneath her when he laughed.

A Lover's Hate

They were cuddled on the front porch swing. The unforgettable beach view was drenched in gold by the setting sun.

"Just thinkin' about you and Georgia lining up to catch the bouquet," Jasper continued to chuckle.

Carmen slapped his arm. "I was the only old fool to take part in that mess. Georgia was nowhere to be found."

Jasper cupped Carmen's jaw and gently directed her face up toward his. "Now why would you think you're an old fool?"

Carmen's lashes settled down over her bright eyes and she offered a simple shrug. "Such things are for young women."

Jasper squeezed her chin, urging her to look at him. "Such things are for *any* woman who dreams of a man making her his- *all* his." He cupped her cheek, brushing his thumb near the corner of her eye. "A man like the one you have right here. A man who's loved you all his life." He gave a warning squeeze when she would have looked away. "A man who promised not to ask you to be his again until he'd silenced your demons. That's been done."

Carmen shivered from contentment. "It still doesn't feel like it's done- finished. Still feels unreal."

"Will you let me make you happy now?"

She reached up to brush her hand across his face. "You've never made me *un*-happy."

"Say you'll marry me."

Inching upward, Carmen replaced her hand with her lips brushing his face. "I will," she said.

The kiss that followed was slow and lazy. Three minutes later, they were still indulging in the sweet exchange when the sound of a throat clearing urged them apart. Slowly, the couple disengaged. Jasper kept Carmen close and focused in on the shape framed in sunlight. The body moved closer, coming more into focus.

Carmen didn't look up at Jasper, but she could feel him tense. His hand had tightened on her shoulder.

"Apologies for interrupting, Sir," said the young man on the other side of the porch. "You said if it was of dire importance…"

Jasper only nodded, too curious about the unexpected arrival of his associate to do much else.

Oscar Navarro glanced toward Carmen and smiled before looking back to his boss. "Sir?"

Jasper ignored the question. "What's happened?" He asked instead.

"Just received word, Sir. Gram Walters is…" he looked to Carmen again, "he's passed away, Sir."

Carmen inched away from Jasper then. She reciprocated Oscar's smile and then waved toward one of the lounge chairs on the porch. "Why don't you have a seat and I'll bring out some iced tea."

Jasper straightened on the swing while Oscar claimed a spot leaning along the porch railing.

"What happened?" Jasper asked.

"He was found dead, Sir." Oscar's brown eyes were as void of emotion as his voice.

"Another car accident?"

"His throat was cut."

Jasper's mouth thinned grimly as he processed the information. "Was the same evidence found at the scene?"

Oscar nodded. "Same that they found with Chappell's body."

Jasper left the swing and walked a slow lap around the porch.

A Lover's Hate

"Is someone coming after us, Sir?" Oscar's eyes were riveted on his boss.

Jasper managed a smile. "Not after you, son. If I'm not mistaken about the motive, this is about something that was before your time."

"What's the motive, Sir?"

Jasper's warm gaze appeared haunted. "Revenge."

***

Smoak relaxed against the doorjamb when Sabra answered the penthouse bell. The half-smile he wore triggered the provocative dent in his cheek.

"Was I unclear about what we were going to do?" he asked.

Sabra shrugged. "You said a walk around the grounds."

"Mmm hmm, operative word- grounds."

Again, she shrugged.

Smoak had to laugh then. It had always been so easy for her to endear herself to him. He acknowledged that she still possess the ability. He recalled their first meeting. Thoughts settled on the first day of classes during their undergrad years. She arrived late, loaded down with shopping bags and no qualms about interrupting the advanced economics class she appeared completely unprepared for. She had the attention of everyone in the room- certainly the attention of every male.

She had always been a knockout- face and body equally captivating. She'd taken an empty desk seat next to him and asked if he'd mind scooting down one seat to make room for her bags. Apparently perturbed, the professor remarked on how nice it was of her to join them. She had the nerve to thank the man in her brightest tone, which only perturbed the instructor further. By the end of the lecture however, Sabra Ramsey had proven she was more than a knockout face and X-rated body.

Smoak recalled how amazed he and his fellow classmates were by her mastery of the subject. The same went for their professor who was smitten by her from then on.

Returning to the present, Smoak pushed off the jamb and flicked his fingers against the dangling ruby earrings Sabra wore with a scandalously tight black tank top emblazoned with its own ruby encrusted design. Black jeans molded to her generous hips and thighs, accentuating her very full derriere. Wedge heeled ruby red boots completed the flashy ensemble.

"Don't you have any sneakers?" Smoak asked her.

"What for?" Sabra scrunched her face as though she found the idea offensive.

Smoak shook his head. "Course not," The woman was as at home in spiked heels as a ballplayer was in cleats, he thought.

"Are we ready or are you gonna stand around critiquing my wardrobe all night?"

Smoak raised his hands and moved back from the door, allowing her to step into the hall.

"I don't understand the point of this," Sabra mumbled.

"You might like to know where the construction'll be taking place when we talk to Ty and her people tomorrow."

Sabra rolled her eyes and set off at her sauntering pace. "So nice of you to talk to me about building this thing *before* you went and put all this shit in place."

"Oh you mean like you talked to me about wanting to build some kind of hedonist spa behind the towers?"

A Lover's Hate

Sabra's back stiffened and she turned. "Damn that Lee Lee," she growled.

"Yeah, I ran into her before I got here. She was near Natalie's desk."

"Oh, she was near Natalie's desk, huh?" Sabra made sure he heard her phony sweetness. She wasn't at all surprised that the man was already on a first name basis with her staff.

"Let's get this over with," she grumbled and brushed past him while attempting to ignore his laughter.

***

"Fascinating. This is absolutely fascinating. I can't believe I haven't taken time before to stand out here in the hot ass sun and get sand blown into my eyes."

"Oh I'm sorry Sabe, aren't your sunglasses working?" Smoak intentionally misread Sabra's sarcasm and grinned when she turned to him without a smile. He knew her gaze was bland behind the designer frames.

As Smoak walked on ahead; sharing his plans for the project and Tykira's part in the transportation design, Sabra's interest peaked. She wouldn't admit it but the plan wasn't as invasive as she'd expected. The portion of the property to be used wouldn't affect the view of the towers from any angle. Still, she held onto mock attitude and appeared unimpressed by what was to come.

"Since it looks like I have no say, I'll just leave it at 'congrats'." With a lazy wave, she headed back to the Jeep Smoak had used to drive them out to the site. She was halfway to the vehicle when he caught her.

"Smoak-"

"No. Listen to me. This," he tilted his head toward the uncultivated property at his back, "this is a means to an end. I need to know what changed with you- it's something and it was clear as day on your face when you looked at me that morning." He tugged her elbow when she attempted to turn away.

"I know getting you to tell me what the hell is going on will be near to impossible, but you know I won't give up. I can't Sabra, not when so much of this is my fault."

She was shaking her head. "It wasn't."

"I'm sorry and I know that's pathetic but it's all I've got aside from being here for you. But to do that I need to know what I'm dealing with."

"Smoak," she pressed her fingers to his mouth. "Stop. You don't have a thing to make up for."

"How can you say that?" his expression was as fierce as his whisper.

"This isn't about what you think," she gasped when he jerked her again and far more roughly than before.

"Then tell me what it's about then!"

Tears sprouted suddenly and she covered her mouth with both hands.

"Christ," something changed in Smoak's expression. "It started before, didn't it?" He bent a little to stare more directly into her face.

Sabra kept her face averted.

"It started before I raped you-"

"You didn't." She shook her head frantically. "It wasn't- you didn't do that."

He was quiet for a long moment. "Was it Brogue?"

Her frantic head shaking continued.

"Did something happen when you were with him? Before you were with me?"

"Stop…" She was crying heavily then. "Smoak don't…"

A Lover's Hate

He relented, loosening his hold on her elbow and massaging her there. "Shh…" he kissed her forehead. "It's alright, it's alright…" he held her tight while she trembled against him. "Let's get you back," he said, tucking her closer for the walk back to the car.

ELEVEN

The next day, Sabra was finishing up her morning rounds with a visit to the cook staff for one of thirty or so restaurants housed inside the resort. She was leaving the final meeting; with a plate of breakfast quiches in hand, when she saw a familiar face across the dining room.

"Miss Imani?" She called once she'd made her way across the pink and lavender dining space of Sabra's Brunch. "Good morning," she leaned down to hug the woman and brushed a kiss across her cheek. "Are you finding everything alright? Everything accessible enough?"

"Oh yes, yes everything's as efficient and lovely as you are."

A Lover's Hate

Sabra tossed her head; not bothering to deny how much the compliment pleased her. "I do my best," she sighed in a playful manner.

"Well your best is exceptional. As exceptional as that wedding you gave my son and daughter-in-law." Imani settled back to trail her fingers across the cowl neck of her elegant dark mocha top as she watched Sabra accept another compliment.

"Well…" Sabra shrugged her brows and gave a saucy toss of her head. "I think everyone was pleased. Hopefully the honeymoon'll be as fantastic as the wedding." Sabra let just a hint of doubt drift across her maple face. "They should've just stayed here." She referred to the newlyweds who had left Las Vegas earlier that morning for the Swiss chalet that Belle's father Jasper Stone had given as his present.

Imani laughed. "I'm sure they enjoyed their time here too, love. Maybe not as much privacy as they would have liked with all sides of their family almost in full attendance."

"You're probably right," Sabra smoothed the scalloped hem of the mallard blue halter dress beneath her and took a seat at the intimate table for two.

Imani sipped her blueberry tea and smiled contentedly. "I can't tell you how lovely it is to have three of my sons under the same roof at the same time."

Sabra's laughter held traces of nervousness. "That must've been quite a surprise for you."

"Oh love it was." Imani sipped more of the tea and then glanced Sabra's way before looking back into her cup. "I suppose you were surprised as well. Seeing Smoak."

Sabra shifted on the pink satin cushion of the chair she occupied. Unsuccessfully, she tried to brush off the nagging shivers that surfaced whenever Smoak's name was mentioned.

"Perhaps you'll be planning another wedding before the year is out." Imani intentionally ignored the younger woman's unease.

"Oh?" Sabra cleared her throat. "So you and Mr. Rome are renewing your vows, huh?"

Imani's laughter was full and instant. She had always enjoyed Sabra's biting quick wit on the few occasions they'd had the chance to talk.

"I was thinking of you and my son." She said once her laughter quieted.

"Miss Imani," Sabra fidgeted with a halter strap of the dress's bra styled bodice and then decided to be blunt. "I'm afraid that really isn't in the cards for us. Ever."

"So certain," Imani noted in a quiet tone of admiration. "That must come in handy when running a business like this. Doesn't always work so well when a relationship is the topic."

"I'm not at my best around him, Miss Immi."

"That only means you don't see the need to put on airs. You can be yourself."

Sabra directed her eyes toward the table as she shook her head. "That's not it." Finally she met Imani's steady gaze. "I can talk to any man about anything and have his jaw dropping over what I know. Your son can sit across from me in silence or he can quote from centuries old texts and *I'd* do good to remember the lyrics of the latest song they're blastin' twenty-four seven on the radio."

Imani had to set aside her tea then, knowing she'd wind up laughing too much to finish.

"I'm sorry for being gruff."

A Lover's Hate

"Don't do that," Imani reached over to squeeze Sabra's clutched hands. "Why are you afraid to show him who you really are?"

"Because I'm afraid he'll see too much." Sabra stunned herself by sharing that, but realized she was gradually tiring of keeping her *secrets*. "They're things he can never know. Things I can't share with anybody."

"Don't you think he might want to share in whatever's troubling you?"

"It not that," Sabra shook her head as though flustered by all that roamed inside it. "This is complicated," she groaned.

Imani reached for her tea cup again. "I understand."

Sabra frowned, watching as the woman calmly sipped the drink. "Aren't you gonna tell me that complications don't matter?"

Imani smiled and her exquisitely shaped eyes narrowed mysteriously. "Sometimes they are *all* that matter. But Sabra, *you* will have to decide if a life with my son is possible if you share your secrets. Will you be stronger for it? Or happier not knowing? Personally, I think Smoak will continue to live a half-life the longer he denies himself one with you."

Sabra blinked, grimacing when she felt moisture pressuring her eyes. "Thank you, Miss Immi." Her tone was uncharacteristically demure then.

"Anytime," Imani squeezed Sabra's hand again, and then winked. "Think you can keep up with me in this thing?" She gestured toward the tech savvy chair she got around in.

Sabra laughed and collected her emotions. "I can give it a try."

The two left the restaurant in high spirits as they chatted up a new subject.

***

Edinburg, Scotland~

Darby Ellis DeBurgh pushed the door shut with her rump and leaned back against the towering slab of mahogany for a few moments to soak in the quiet of the suite. The Muir Inn had been her home close to two weeks. She and her husband had been like ships passing in the night for months.

Kraven was growing busier everyday it seemed with the remodeling of the castle for the hunting lodge in Near Invernesshire. Not one to sit around resting on her laurels, Darby chose not to let her considerable PR skills go to waste.

As Lord and Lady DeBurgh, the couple lived up to their responsibilities to the visitors they entertained. Many of those visitors had turned into new and lucrative clients for Darby. Acquaintances of the DeBurgh family were delighted to find the estate renewed with love and life. Of course acquaintances and members of the extended DeBurgh clan were more than a little curious about the new lady of the manor.

Darby kicked off one of her stylish navy platform pumps and hobbled over to the credenza where the mail waited. Though mail delivery wasn't an amenity provided by the five-star inn; where Kraven kept an apartment, it was a service graciously and happily offered to the lovely Lady DeBurgh. She had charmed the staff before the onset of her third day on the premises.

She took the most interesting piece- a fashion magazine- and made her way to the sofa. She was about to

A Lover's Hate

pull off the other shoe, when commotion rose from the staircase leading to the bedroom loft. Darby had only a second to wait for the source of the noise to be revealed.

The fashion magazine fell from suddenly limp fingers when Darby saw her husband descending the stairs. But for the white bath sheet knotted at his waist, his massive sun-kissed frame was nude and sparkled with beads of water.

"Apologies, Lass. I was hoping to be done with my shower by the time you got home."

Darby remained still in the middle of the living room. One shoe off and one shoe on, her tote strap barely clung to her wrist.

"You're here."

Kraven DeBurgh's brilliant emerald gaze twinkled appealingly when he laughed over his wife's awed tone of voice.

"Aye," he said, using a smaller towel to mop the heart-stopping face framed by damp ebony waves.

"And so are you," he murmured upon closing the distance between them. "And it's about time, too. I wanted to take my shower with you."

Darby was still bewildered and in utter disbelief that he was there. "Why…" She couldn't finish her question.

"Because I bloody miss you, that's why." He relieved her of the tote she carried.

Darby wasted no more time trying to ask questions. She threw herself against his broad, sleek chest and they were kissing madly seconds later. Kraven pulled her high against him. Imprisoning her neck in his hand, he deepened the slow strokes of his tongue.

Darby was frantic to get out of the pearl gray suit she'd worn that day. Kraven already had her out of the skirt and was then at work on the half-slip and hose beneath it.

"Why are you here?" Darby was finally able to finish the questions while she pressed fast, moist kisses to his mouth. "I thought you couldn't get away to come with me."

"Well you've got Hadrian to thank for that- in part anyway."

"What?" She laughed at Kraven's mention of his beloved horse. Kraven had bent to pull the hose from her legs and she braced her hands to his back, at once enthralled by the flexing muscles beneath his richly tanned skin.

"Well we were out for a morning ride when it occurred to Hadrian what an idiot I was being to let you come here on your own."

"Hmph. Hadrian's getting smarter every day."

Kraven straightened and grinned down at his wife. "Damn straight," he shrugged playfully. "But I can't give him all the credit. A call came in from County and Fernando before I left."

The news intrigued Darby and she waited on her husband to explain.

"The newlyweds are headed to Paris for the last leg of their honeymoon. They wanted to know if we could all get together." He faked a look of indifference. "I figured we could use a little time in Paris."

Darby squealed in his arms. "When are we going?"

"Well it'll be a few weeks yet before they get there."

"Oh." Darby's mouth curved down in disappointment. "So when do you have to go back home?"

A Lover's Hate

He gave her a little bounce. "When you can go home with me."

The brightness returned to her honey-toned face then. "Three weeks," she sighed and smoothed her hands along the chorded length of his arms. "What are we gonna do with all that time?"

"Why Lady DeBurgh," he pulled her off her feet and carried her toward the staircase. "I thought you'd never ask."

***

"So what's your idiot husband got to say about your gorgeous crew being out here and fawning all over you?" Sabra teased when she linked arms with Tykira and pulled her toward the other side of the office.

"He's finally gotten used to them," Ty laughed. "I'm really proud of his progress."

"Hmm…" Sabra scrunched her nose. "Somehow *progress* and *Quaysar Ramsey* sound wrong together."

The two women were deep in the throes of laughter when Smoak arrived. Ty went over for hugs and kisses and introduced her team before Smoak did the same introducing the senior staff of his lab. While the crews exchanged handshakes and got better acquainted, Smoak went to Sabra.

"You okay?" He asked once they'd claimed a quiet corner of the room. He seemed satisfied by the nod she gave and then he patted her waist encouragingly. "Come on and meet the folks who kicked you out of your office."

Sabra; who had been less than enthused by the upcoming construction on her property, had found more to approve of regarding the project. Tykira and her crew came with blueprints as well as a scale model of the proposed result.

The light rail looked like some sort of silver bullet zipping over, through and around the resort. This was something the other boys on the block didn't have, Sabra celebrated the fact. Oh yes, she was liking this more and more.

"Of course the final design will depend on the architects and contractors final plans for the new lab facility," Ty was saying while twisting to and fro in the cream swivel chair she'd claimed in the middle of the table. "And Lee Lee says we're still waiting on some building permits."

"Just a little red tape," Lee made a few last notes in her portfolio. "We'll be ready to roll by the time everyone's ready to break ground," she assured her boss.

Sabra was already thinking of the monetary reward the new toy could bring. "So is this thing just for Smoak and his people or can I offer it as a perk to some of my high rollers?"

"Well it'll be a luxurious piece of equipment, no doubt." Ty tugged the cuff of her black shortwaist blazer and smirked. "Luckily, I only have to build the thing. You and Smoak will have to compromise on how you'll want to use it."

Sabra looked toward her 'partner' and didn't know what to make of the unreadable glint in his unsettling eyes.

Trish Hashway was on her way out of the office. The young, secretarial assistant had been taking the minutes of the meeting between Ty, Smoak and Sabra.

"How's that baby boy, Trish?" Sabra asked before the young woman left the room.

"Oh he's great, Ms. Ramsey. Putting on pounds like a heavyweight," the new mother raved.

A Lover's Hate

"Heard anything from Hart?" Sabra referred to the father who had walked out on Trish and his son two months prior.

Trish shook her head firmly. "No ma'am."

"How's that sitter?" Sabra rested one hand to her hip, the other to the back of one of the swivel chairs at the table.

Trish's dimming expression was luminous again. "Oh she's great. Everything's been terrific Ms. Ramsey. They called this morning to tell me the apartment was ready. I can't thank you enough for what you've done."

"Then don't, that's not why I did it."

"No ma'am."

Smoak smiled from his place near the end of the table. He observed the young woman who looked ready to shed tears from happiness.

"There's only one key," Sabra was saying, "I'll be very upset if I hear that jackass boyfriend of yours has one if he decides to show his no good face."

"Thank you Ms. Ramsey. I won't let you down."

Sabra waved a hand. "I know you won't. Now get out of here," she faked a harsh tone of voice, but winked to send Trish on her way.

"That was decent." Smoak noted.

Sabra looked nonchalant. "Not everyone can afford nannies 'round the clock like my mother could." She said.

"Well it was decent."

Sabra waved a hand this time. "It was necessary."

"And decent."

She shrugged.

Smoak could tell she was embarrassed, so he relented. "Am I mistaken or are you not as against this project as you were?"

"Rail's pretty cool. Wish I had thought of it." She strolled along the closest end of the table.

"Think we can co-exist here?"

"Co-exist for how long?" She leaned over the back of one of the swivel chairs. "Do you actually want to live here?"

He shrugged.

"Get the fuck out."

"You don't believe me?"

"Not a bit."

"Why?"

"Because it's Vegas. This isn't your cup of tea."

"You're my cup of tea." He said with a straight face.

"Smoak…" Closing her eyes, she leaned back her head. "Haven't we hurt each other enough?"

"Damn right we have. Don't you think it's time we stopped?"

It occurred to her then that they were alone. The meeting attendees had cleared out most quietly. The quietness of others had nothing to do with it though, she was simply so absorbed in the gaze, stance and mere presence of the man she loved, that everything else fell away.

"Brogue's here, Smoak. We can't ignore that- can't ignore what that means to us. And he's still a friend to me." She kept her toffee gaze direct. "But that's *all* he's been since…that night. I swear."

A slow smile broke past his closed expression.

She pressed her lips together, briefly hesitating over her next words. "You've got to stop blaming yourself for what happened then."

His smiled wavered. "Why should I?"

A Lover's Hate

"Smoak, I was a mess a long time before that day- a long time before that night with Brogue."

"Alright, alright," his brows drew into a slight frown as he waved at her words. Despite wanting to get to the bottom of what was happening with her, the idea of her with Brogue- remembering the sight of them together still made him livid.

Sabra was lost in her own regrets and paid little attention to his reactions. "Whatever you… think is going on, it's not about Brogue or you."

"Sabra…" He stopped her pacing, stepping in her path and bringing her against him. "Stop. Stop this now… Do you think what you're saying is going to sway me? Make me not want to find out what's going on with you?"

He was kissing her before she could answer and she was melting sweetly into his chest. The lull of conversation beyond the office walls, didn't give them reason for caution. Smoak tugged her with him to the desk where he settled to the corner.

Sabra kneaded his broad, muscular thighs set on either side of her body. Throaty moans escaped her the entire while his tongue wrestled with hers. Smoak remedied the confinements of the bra-styled bodice of her dress with one simple tug of his hand. The scene grew more explosive and Sabra wasn't of a mind to resist anything he did.

"Come to me later." He spoke during the ravenous thrusts of his tongue.

"Whatever you want," she managed, pressing more of a bared breast into his palm.

He broke the kiss then. "You mean that?" He brushed his thumb across her nipple and followed the move with his black eyes. "I mean to have the truth. Whatever it is. Do you understand me?"

AlTonya Washington

Sabra nodded like an obedient student. She was only interested in having more of his kisses. "Can I come with you now?" She didn't care how she sounded; she was on fire for him. Her fingers curved tightly into the crisp material of his shirt. "Please? I need you."

The whispered beg was Smoak's undoing. The desk would serve their purposes nicely.

TWELVE

"You do realize your door isn't locked?"

"Screw it. Don't stop."

Smoak chuckled, joy and arousal fueling the gesture. It was indeed a rush to drive such a woman insane with need. She commanded so much, demanded much of her staff. Yet she handled it all with a no-nonsense air and a gruffness that was so clearly at odds with her soft heart. He'd never stopped loving her, but she was making him fall *in* love with her all over again.

"We need to stop, Sweet," he managed, drawing her hair back away from her face to secure it in a loose hold. "This is your office."

"My apartment's just on the other side," she bartered, ignoring the logic of his words. Hungrily, she suckled his nipples visible once she'd opened his shirt. Her soft wet kisses traveled lower, massaging his sex- long and hard beneath his trousers.

Smoak tugged her back up and lost himself in the fragrant valley past her bodice. He merely inhaled her scent instead of feasting on her the way he wanted. Her hips nudged his insistently while she sat astride him on the desk. She began to undo his pants and his hand imprisoned her wrist.

"Smoak," she pleaded.

"Someone might need you," he reasoned while wickedness flooded his expression.

Sabra rolled her eyes. "Forget them, fuck me…" she whined.

His laughter filled the room and; in a display of sheer willpower he denied what they were both starving for. He pushed off his back, maintaining a possessive grip about her hips lest she topple off him.

"You know where I'm staying. Come see me at seven." His steady gaze brooked no argument. He bumped her jaw once with his fist and waited until she lifted her chin and sighed to unwillingly accept his wishes.

Still, she tried to entice him into something to sustain her when he dropped a quick kiss to her mouth. Smoak wouldn't be tempted and brushed his lips across her cheek before setting her away and leaving the office.

Sabra waited until she was alone and then relaxed back down on her desk. Silently, she ordered a stop to the frenzy of sensation between her thighs. When a measure of relief stirred, she inched off the cluttered desktop and tested the strength of her legs by strolling around the room as she fixed her clothes. A few paces in, she brought a hand to her mouth and felt the smile there.

AlTonya Washington

"Ah dammit Sabra, stop!" She said, knowing she was acting like a sap.

Work was the key and she turned her focus back to the desk where a suede date book lay open. It was the

regular print kind she preferred over Lee Lee's electronic gadgets.

She was scanning for her next appointment when she felt the card in the side pocket of her dress. Frowning, she withdrew it and realized what she held.

"Damn," she muttered and hurried out.

Imani was seated before a wide work desk in the bedroom suite. Her laughter rang out in response to something her father said about the world not being a place for old men. Imani watched her father frowning into the web cam as they communicated. Her laughter bubbled up again.

"You're wrong, Papa. You're not an old man. You're an old Chief."

Hillar Kamande fought to maintain a stony demeanor but he was betrayed by the smile spreading across his handsome molasses dark face.

"You should not gloat," Hillar advised his youngest child.

"Oh…" Imani waved a hand before the laptop screen. "You're at least allowed to be happy. After all, doesn't Hillar mean cheerful?" She challenged.

Hillar Kamande had just been given the honor of Chief in the Mozambique village he hailed from when an elder brother stepped aside. As the youngest of five sons, Hillar was expected to assume the duty.

His laughter was abrupt and highly contagious. "You sound like your mother now," he referenced his wife Isis.

"And speaking of names," the camera captured Hill's jerky movements as he folded long beefy arms across the black and brown sweater vest he wore. "You've spoken of all my boys except Hill. Did he attend the wedding?"

"If he was there, I didn't know." Imani couldn't mask the sadness in her voice or expression.

"Foolish boy," Hillar chastised his grandson yet his granite voice was softened by affection. "He'll come around one day, lovely girl."

Imani tried and failed to produce a smile. "I used to believe that."

"You should never have joined the names." Hillar suddenly snapped. "Liam, must mean idiot."

Imani laughed over the dig at her late father-in-law. "Well it was only fair for Roman's father to be represented too. Hill was his first grandson and *you* did get the first part of the name after all."

Hillar chuckled then. "And how is my son-in-law?"

Imani drew the cashmere wrap about her shoulders and smiled satisfactorily. "Very good- enjoying time with his brother and friends. And what about you two? Still enjoying your holiday?" Hillar and Isis Kamande were visiting Cape Town, South Africa.

Hillar grunted. "Place is too much for me. Not a world for old men, lovely girl. Not a world for old men, at all."

***

AlTonya Washington

Seattle, Washington~

"So everything's alright? You're certain?" Drake Reinard's probe regarded the report he'd just received.

"Was my message unclear?" Quest spoke in the direction of the phone while dropping change from his jeans to a cup on the bedroom dresser.

"No..." From his office halfway around the world, Drake flipped through the hefty document set atop his desk. "It just didn't have that feeling of total um...certainty I've come to expect from you."

Quest grinned, dumping an entire overnight case of socks and boxer shorts into the hamper he'd pulled from his side of the wardrobe room. He and Michaela had just returned from Las Vegas. While unpacking, Quest decided a call was warranted to his Chief Operating Officer at Ramsey World Headquarters in Sion, Switzerland.

"Are you trying to tell me I'm indecisive, Drake?"

Laughter held a distinct undercurrent to Quest's inquiry and soon Drake was giving into the gesture.

"Not at all," he chuckled while wiping laugh tears from his eyes. "But I know there were questions about a few things in the report."

"Yeah..." Quest's mouth thinned into a grim line that triggered his left dimple. He thought of his conversation with Pike, Caiphus and Smoak over their brother's large weapons purchases.

"I'm good with everything." He said.

Drake sighed after a moment. "Does that mean you'd like for me to stop looking into the payouts from your uncle's stock?"

A Lover's Hate

Quest halted midway to the closet to deposit the overnight case. He'd forgotten that he'd asked Drake to chase down that loose thread.

"It's probably nothin'." He muttered, stopping to collect one of Quincee's rag dolls peeking out from beneath the dresser.

"You may be right. There's been no activity there since those last few payments just after your uncle's death."

"Right..." Quest was still stooping before the dresser. His mouth curved faintly as he studied the frayed knobby edges of the doll's arms and legs. "Could be nothin'..."

Drake sighed on a chuckle. "Right then...so I'll tell you when I've got something, eh?"

Grinning broadly again, Quest tapped the doll against his palm. "Thanks for knowing my mind."

"Anytime. Oh! And Quest-"

"I know and I want to be told- whatever you find."

"Right. Kiss your ladies for me, will you?" The connection silenced.

Quest studied his daughter's toy a few more seconds before tossing it to the bed and leaning back on the dresser. Agitation took hold of his expression then.

Brogue grinned when the petite Asian waitress set down the drink he'd ordered. "Have you been assigned as my personal bartender?" he asked.

"You could say that," the woman smiled. "Ms. Ramsey's number one rule is that we make the customer wish he'd never have to leave."

"Ah..." Brogue's laughter was soft. "I thought Ms. Ramsey's number one rule was to never let the customer leave with money in his pockets."

Server and guest shared a long laugh at their hostess' expense.

"Thank you," Brogue turned the glass on the napkin beneath it. "Join me?"

"Well…"

Brogue pushed a foot against the chair across from him. It slid away from the table as a silent indication for the woman to have a seat.

"I haven't even asked your name." He said when the Asian beauty took the chair.

"Rain," she replied.

"Brogue," he offered his hand for a shake.

"Vegas isn't a place to look so downtrodden," Rain noted after she and Brogue had enjoyed a lighter conversation to become better acquainted. "You don't strike me as the kind of man who can't handle himself in the pits."

Brogue laughed again while silently acknowledging that the woman may never have been more right.

"Which means you must be here trying to get over a woman."

"You gather all that from my expression."

Rain's shoulder rose beneath the black halter blouse of her uniform. "I'm very good at reading people. In my business, I have to be."

"Hmph," Brogue nodded as if he accepted the validity of her explanation. "You may be right. About it being a woman- but it's not what you think. It's not about a broken heart."

"Perhaps not for her."

"No," Brogue's laughter held a more robust element then. "No, not for her…"

Rain leaned in over the table. "Have you told her how you feel?"

Brogue lifted the glass but didn't take a sip. "She's got some idea, but we both know it can't work. She's not for me."

Creases formed across Rain's delicate brow. "I wouldn't have pegged you for one to give up."

"I'm a firm believer in fate. There's no stoppin' it." He downed some of the bourbon then.

"Fate," Rain rested her chin on her palm and appeared to be turning the word over in her mind. "Time can be a powerful opponent of it, you know?"

"She belongs to my cousin. Always has. Even when she thought they were done- even then, she was his."

"That doesn't seem fair. I guess your cousin is a powerful opponent of fate as well."

Brogue selected that moment to look up. His bright eyes narrowed and he nodded once while raising his glass in toast. "Rain my love, he most certainly is that." He said and stared across the bar at Smoak.

"Miss Imani?"

Sabra knocked once more on the door to the Tesanos villa. She waited a second or two longer and then figured Imani was already napping. Using the key in hand, Sabra let herself in.

Their earlier conversation had ended with Sabra escorting Imani back to the split level villa. She'd forgotten to leave the key which she realized upon feeling it in her pocket.

"Miss Imani? Mr. Rome?" Sabra gave pause, considering the fact that she could have been... interrupting them. Quickly, she tipped through the foyer and into the

AlTonya Washington

living room. There, she scribbled a quick note to Imani about the key.

Hillar Kamande had requested a good old fashioned phone conversation instead of a tech savvy web chat with his daughter.

Sabra was making a hasty exit out of the living room when she heard Imani's voice. The woman was on the phone with her father. Imani Tesano was on the phone and *walking* out into the living room.

THIRTEEN

"Father I'll have to call you back." Imani said her goodbyes and then clicked off the phone and tossed it to the maroon loveseat just inside the room.

The sound of Sabra's ragged breathing filled the air for a long time. Imani stood still, waiting for Sabra's brain to believe what her eyes were telling her.

Sabra's eyes and brain however had taken up opposing sides of the situation. Sabra shook her head wildly as though there was no way what she saw could be real.

"Miss Imani- what the hell?!" She gushed.

Moving quickly, Imani grabbed Sabra's wrist and kept hold of it while dragging the young woman behind her. In the foyer, she set the bolt on the door and pulled a high backed chair in front of it.

A Lover's Hate

Next, she tugged Sabra back into the living room and pushed her onto the sofa. Imani took a seat on the coffee table.

Sabra's expressive eyes were wide and roamed Imani's legs that were hidden beneath a gold silk robe.

"You will not speak of this." Imani's voice was as calm and regal as ever.

"But how-?"

"Sabra. You will *not* speak of this."

Sabra shook her head as if it pained her to do so. "Smoak-"

"You cannot tell him this."

"What?" Sabra's gasp mirrored the disbelief in her expression. "He already despises me for what's happened between us. If he finds out I know this...he'll hate me forever."

Imani smiled. "Listen to me love, right now you and I are the only two people in this hemisphere who know I can walk."

"Mr. Rome?"

Imani shook her head and bowed it for a few moments. "Roman swore he'd kill the person who put me in that chair. I can't have him find out and go off...doing something insane. Right now, it's only the two of us and my family who know the truth." She leaned close to squeeze Sabra's hands.

"I'm so sorry, love. I know this is difficult and unfair of me to ask given that you two are trying to work things out."

Sabra blinked, her full oval face a picture of hope. "Did he say that?"

Laughing then, Imani cupped Sabra's cheeks and gave them a pat. "You strong, beautiful girl. I can see why my Smoak doesn't know whether he's coming or going when it comes to you."

"He's too good." Sabra swallowed down emotion threatening to block her throat. "I don't deserve him."

Imani smoothed wayward strands of hair from Sabra's cheek. "You do even when you don't think you do."

"You don't know what I've done. How I hurt him."

Serenely, Imani smiled. "I'm blessed in that my sons share things with me especially things related to their love lives."

"He told you," Sabra's voice was faint as she frowned. It was easy to read the look Imani gave in response.

"God," Mortified, Sabra left the sofa wrapping her arms about her chilled body. Shaking and feeling mildly ill, she went to stare blindly past the drapes which were partly drawn to reveal the strip. Suddenly a humorless rip of laughter belted past her lips.

"Now I get it," she sent Imani a stale look. "You guess I think it's okay to hide this, right? Should be easy for me after deceiving him with his cousin."

Imani left the coffee table. "You're no fool Sabra so please don't talk like one." She kept her hands on Sabra's arms when she would have turned away.

"Do you believe I think less of you for that?"

"I hurt him."

"And he hurt you. Now the two of you must find a way past that."

Swallowing again, Sabra felt that faint nauseous feeling rising up once more. "I wonder if there *is* a way past all this."

"Is that what you want?"

A Lover's Hate

"What I *want*? Hmph," Scowling deeply, Sabra folded her arms across the provocative bodice of her dress. "I learned a long time ago not to put my stock in wants."

"Then put your stock in trust," Imani countered, her elegant features set sternly. "Trust in the fact that my son loves you and that he protects what's his. He protects with a fierceness. He's been that way since he was a child. He'll do what he must to keep safe what he treasures." Imani paused to take a breath and rest her forehead against her fingers.

"I believe that Sabra. I believe it or else I wouldn't be here asking you to forget what you've seen here today."

Sabra nodded finally. "I won't tell him. But will *you* ever tell them? They have to be sick out of their minds with worry over you after all this time." Indignation pooled in her toffee colored eyes. "It just doesn't seem right for you to hide this, is all."

"What's right is protecting my husband," Imani said even though she looked as if she admired the young woman who challenged her. "I can't let Roman run off to torture and kill his brother for paralyzing me when it wasn't his brother who did this."

"They were all hits." Brogue tossed back his fresh drink and winced as the liquid burned its way through his torso. He'd contacted his cousin and asked for the long overdue meeting.

"The contracts weren't taken out by my father though." He finished.

Smoak tapped his fingers to the rim of the glass he claimed. "I can understand Yvonne, Cufi maybe even Houston but why Daphne Ramsey?"

"I don't ask questions," Brogue drew a hoard of lush wheat colored waves back from his face. "And you do understand that I can't say who hired me."

Smoak finally indulged in a generous swallow of the bourbon Brogue had ordered him. "I could torture it out of you."

Brogue chuckled over the coolly delivered threat. "You'd have to wait in line for that honor," he shrugged, "but I guess that'd put you at the front of the line anyway, so have at it."

Smoak couldn't resist chuckling then. For a time, the cousins laughed like old friends. The sight was quite unique since murderous intentions so often flourished on either side.

Brogue was first to sober somewhat from the laugh attack. "She wasn't herself that night, Smoak. She wasn't drunk, but she wasn't herself. Something was off and- later I just let her think that she'd been drinking and I…"

Smoak focused on the remaining liquid in his glass. "I need to hear it."

"No you don't. You don't want to hear that I've wanted her since the first day I met her or that I took full advantage of the opportunity to have her. Right," Brogue watched Smoak's jaw muscles flex as his anger mounted.

"She thought I was you…later-before you found us. She woke up and called me by your name." Brogue could feel his own jaw muscles flexing then. "She thought I was you and I took what she thought she was giving to you and then you found us.

To tell you the truth, I don't think she knew who anybody was. She was definitely out of it when I got there."

A Lover's Hate

Smoak fought to breathe past the emotion filling his lungs. "How do you know that?" he managed to ask.

Brogue considered his answer for a split second. "I guess it was the fact that she was wearing some kind of lacy, skimpy piece of nothing she might wear to bed. That gave it away plus she was on her way out like she was fully dressed. When she opened the door to me it was like she was expecting me- not *me* personally just… I guess she figured I'd do.

I swear I didn't go there intending to sleep with her." Brogue ventured the explanation once silence had lingered beyond half a minute. He grinned but the gesture held no humor. "I'd sound like a fuckin' buffoon if I said she forced herself on me or that I just couldn't fight her off. Hmph…" he paused to stroke his jaw. "She was very determined though. I honestly don't think I could've gotten out of there without her drawing my blood. Since you're already primed to cut my throat, I may as well tell you that saying no to her was the farthest thing from my mind."

"Why'd you go see her that night?"

"Wanted to check up on her."

"Why?"

"She stopped by my place the night before." Brogue pushed his glass aside. "She didn't know my dad was there, but it was cool. It was still early we could all have dinner or something. But she…" His gaze held a faraway glimmer. "She was different just like that. Then she left. I was on edge about it, so I went to see her that night after dad left."

"What?" Smoak queried when Brogue suddenly shook his head as though he was newly perplexed.

"When you found us that day," he began, "she got up to race after you and the look she gave me- it was like she knew me, but had no clue why I was there."

AlTonya Washington

***

Sabra returned to her apartment still dazed by earlier events. A drink would have been a nice start to calming her fried nerves. A drink however was the last thing she needed to fall back on. What she needed was her bed- her nice *safe* bed.

Imani Tesano could walk and she didn't want her family to know because her husband had vowed to kill the person responsible. Imani swore it wasn't Roman's brother. So who was it? Why was she protecting them?

Sabra had just settled into the first chair she passed when the doorbell chimed. She went to answer and gave a start at finding Smoak on the other side.

He glanced toward the silver timepiece glinting out beneath the cuff of his jacket. "It's past seven."

"I'm sorry I..." She recalled his command from earlier that day. "I didn't forget, something just came up and-"

"Hey, shh...stop," Smoak moved close to prop her chin on his fist. "Forget about it, I'm only teasing. I know how busy you are." Still, the look she gave roused his curiosity. He bumped her chin lightly with the back of his hand.

"What?" He prompted.

"You're just," she blinked as though she were still dazed. "What have you invented down in your lab that adjusted your attitude so nicely?" In truth, the man in her midst was the one she'd only glimpsed on occasion. Smoak had never allowed that part of his persona much stage time. Sabra prayed he was reconsidering keeping that part of himself hidden, because that was the part she'd fallen in love with.

A Lover's Hate

His onyx stare softened in tandem with the sexy lift of his mouth when he shrugged. "Anger and hate are strong. They can send a man railing out against everything in his path. Even those he loves most," he brushed at the tip of a curl disappearing into her cleavage, his fingers were intent on tugging it free.

"Smoak," her voice carried a pleading tone.

"Is this you turning down my earlier request?" He retrieved the curl and moved his fingers reluctantly.

"It's so late."

He laughed. "Is this *you* talking?"

She could think of nothing else to say and silence claimed dominance.

"May I at least come in?" His head tilted at a curious angle when she seemed to hesitate before waving him inside.

"I was just gonna grab something and turn in." She faked an airy tone.

Smoak let the door close softly at his back. "I'd really appreciate you coming out with me tonight."

"Because there're things we still need to discuss."

Smoak only smiled.

A door closed in the distance. Lee Lee was coming down the corridor and only noticed Sabra in her line of sight.

"Oh, it's you girl. I thought I heard the bell. Are you ready for bed?"

Sabra cleared her throat noisily and subtly slid her stare in Smoak's direction.

"Hey Smoak," Lee Lee maintained her unflustered demeanor. "Good to see you."

"We're on our way out," Sabra blurted.

AlTonya Washington

"Well I'll talk to you later then." Lee Lee put a dazzling smile in place. "Night, Smoak."

"Ready?" Sabra inquired once Lee Lee headed off toward the kitchen. She went back to the front door as if going out was her intention all along.

Smoak was slower to move. Curiosity sparkled undeniably in his dark eyes.

There were few places (if any) that Sabra Ramsey could travel within her resort and not be recognized. Such was definitely the case that evening. Smoak had offered his arm shortly after they left her penthouse. He hadn't asked whatever questions lurked in the bottomless recesses of his gaze and Sabra was utterly thankful.

She was even more thankful for the arm he offered. Sabra was so off kilter she could have stumbled easily even as she strolled around in heels that were part of her usual ensemble. Determinedly, she kept hold of Smoak even as her attention was requested from members of her staff and guests.

Men, who would have otherwise flirted outrageously with her, kept their greetings flattering yet subdued in light of the quietly intimidating man she held onto. The women who requested Sabra's time could scarcely share their remarks they were so intent on observing Smoak Tesano.

Alas, the couple finally made it to the table Smoak had secured in the lavish and romantic Sabra's Desire. The establishment was comprised of a series of private dining rooms. Spanish guitar pieces were piped in and encouraged diners to take twirls around glass dance floors lit by electric candlelight. The wait staff was discreet arriving in the dining suites only when they were called.

A Lover's Hate

"What are we doing here?" Sabra spoke through clenched teeth soon after they'd greeted the host who would show them to their suite.

"Figured you'd prefer eating out instead of inside my villa."

"*My* villa is just fine for dining in." Her whisper sounded harsh.

Smoak halted his steps and let the host walk on ahead. Sabra's hand slipped from the crook of his arm but he captured her elbow soon after. His facial muscles were relaxed but his eyes glinted with a warning fire. "I don't really think you're equipped to have an honest to goodness pissin' contest with me."

She moved close enough so that her breasts were bumping his chest. "I'm very good at adapting." She said and had to bite back a smile when he laughed.

"Just use the call box when you want the server, Mr. Tesano." The host instructed once Smoak and Sabra caught up to him in the dining room. The man waved toward the table where the device was located.

"Shall I send someone now or would you prefer to contact them, Sir?"

Smoak offered a casual wave and shook his head. "I'll take care of it."

The host followed through with a stiff bow. "Sir."

"They're trained to speak with the man." Sabra explained at Smoak's inquisitive look. "The woman's supposed to be treated like-"

"She's a non-entity?"

Sabra rolled her eyes. "Like she's here to be pampered and not bothered by trivial concerns like ringing for the server or paying the bill." She fluffed her hair back over her shoulders and sized him up. "If a man brings a woman here, he better have deep pockets and be ready to dig in 'em."

"Hmph. It's a good thing I own half the place."

Again, Sabra rolled her eyes and turned to direct her focus toward the dining room. "Staff's probably already deep in discussion about us. Rumor mill will be goin' full steam. By morning it'll be all over the resort that I'm screwing you." She tapped a manicured thumbnail to her lip and worried.

Smoak approached her on silent steps. His arms snaked possessively about her waist and he drew her in, nibbling the soft flesh of her earlobe. One hand had already risen to cup a breast.

Not much more was needed to entice a response from Sabra. She turned, curving eagerly into him. Her mouth fused against his in a hungry display and she kissed him desperately. Nails raking the sleek hair tapering his nape, she thrust her tongue progressively deeper into his mouth. The need; barely dormant inside her, funneled back into fury and again she was on fire for him. She lost all sense of reason. She even forgot where they were which was obvious when she started to undo the oatmeal heather trousers he wore.

Sound, resembling a clearing throat filled the room. "You called, Mr. Tesano?"

Sabra's hand stilled and she subtly tugged the tanned shirt back in place outside his trousers. She saw the grin Smoak wore as well as the call box he'd picked up as they'd kissed.

"Yeah," he said, laughter in his eyes before he turned them to the server. "Thanks, uh...?" he requested the young man's name.

"Cory, Sir."

"Thanks Cory," still having fun with the situation, Smoak patted Sabra's bottom to send her on her way. "I'll start with a Lager. Sam Adams and uh-babe?" he addressed Sabra. "What'll you have?"

Ignoring Smoak's playful expression, Sabra smiled at the waiter. "Hey Cory, I'll have a ginger ale." She went to stand before the tall windows while Smoak finished up with the server. She forced herself to resist responding when his hands smoothed about her waist again.

"So what's your plan?" She allowed him free reign over her body. His lips skimmed her shoulder and up along her neck. "Gonna have me naked and on my back by the time Cory gets here with the drinks?" It was all she could do to be still and not start kissing him senseless again.

"I don't want you on your back," he cupped her chin and angled it to provide more room for his mouth on her neck. "I prefer to have you standing," he clarified, laughing softly when she weakened next to him. "Sweet, I'm sorry," he finally took mercy. "I swear this isn't about humiliating you in front of your staff. I really do want us someplace where we can talk."

She turned on him then, observing him dubiously for long moments. "Talk? About anything?"

He lowered his head a fraction to nod.

"Alright," she stepped back. The doubt in her long, toffee stare mingled with something else. "Let's talk about your mother's accident."

FOURTEEN

Smoak's head tilted, his features sharpening with suspicions and fierce tendencies. "Why the hell would you want that?"

"I talked to her earlier- Miss Imani." Sabra wrenched her hands and forced herself to continue. "She's so full of life. It's a shame that nothing can be done to get her out of that damn chair."

He blinked. The strained emotion on his face softened into weariness. "I know..." stroking his jaw, he walked the length of the windows that provided the view of the elevated pools extending from the tenth story of the second tower.

"It was a hit and run. Her doctors could never tell us a damn thing. Even though her injuries were extensive, they didn't think she'd be paralyzed for the foreseeable future. We all expected her to be walking by now."

A Lover's Hate

"We weren't on the best terms when it happened. You and I," Sabra moved slowly, closer to him. "I never asked later, how it happened…"

"She went out one day in my dad's truck." He laughed shortly at how simply it all began. "They were getting ready for one of their trips to Mozambique. Dad was home washing her car, she was packing-same routine, taking care of shit at home before they left." The view of the pools grew blurred and Smoak realized his own tears were at fault. Angrily, he swiped at them with the back of his hand.

"She needed to get some stuff from the store- he told her to take the truck. They clipped her the second she passed the gates and cleared the driveway."

"They?" Sabra peeked around trying to assess his expression. She could only see the muscle flexing in his jaw at a furious frantic pace.

"Didn't take much for us to figure it was the family. At least it didn't take much for me and my dad to see it. Nothing was proven. Dad never followed up on it-made us promise not to….and Mama made him promise not to do anything…it's been the hardest thing for any of us to live up to."

He drew a fist, smoothing his palm across it with slow deliberation. "The bastards hated her from the second they met her and saw she couldn't trace her roots back to the old country."

"Italy," Sabra sighed. "They tried to kill her to get her out of your dad's life." She frowned. "But why do it *then*? They'd been married over twenty years."

"Dad thinks it's about him." Smoak worked his fingers over the bridge of his nose. "Says he pissed somebody off and they wanted payback."

"Is he sure it was his family?"

"He's sure it was Gabriel."

Sabra felt her heart drop. Imani hadn't shared the name of which brother her husband held responsible, but somehow she knew. She knew Gabriel was the one. Why would Imani think him incapable of such a thing?

"My turn," Smoak had turned from the windows. His suspicions were back in place. "I talked to Brogue."

Her gaze averted and she accepted the fact that her heart would be swimming in her stomach a little longer. "Guess I don't need to ask about what," she said.

Smoak raised her chin on his index finger. "He said you weren't drunk that night. Off- not drunk." He took her wrists, preventing her from turning away. "He says you were fine when you knocked on his door that day, but by the time you left he knew something was wrong."

Sabra shook her wrists in his hand, but his hold didn't give. "Why is it so important for you to know this?"

"Why is it so important for *me*?" Smoak's clear voice held an incredulous ring. "Are *you* alright thinking you slept with someone because you were drunk when you weren't? Brogue told me how you were- that morning after I left. He said you looked at him like you had no idea what happened."

She managed to break free of his hold then. "Did it occur to either of you *geniuses* that I was mortified over what happened? Over what I did? Our relationship wasn't prefect Smoak but it was everything to me. *You* were everything to me. I was a fool for you even though you never trusted me- never trusted me enough to share with me what ate away at you…closed you off to me when I least expected it." Bumps riddled her bare arms, but she ignored the chill.

A Lover's Hate

"What happened between us that afternoon was probably the most honest thing that had ever happened between us."

The dining room bell punctuated her admission. Their drinks had arrived.

"They hated me from the day I was born, Sabra." He shared his own admission once the waiter left. "They hated me because of this," one hand grazed the chorded column of his neck, across the taut onyx skin that covered it.

"My grandfather Liam liked my mother- thought she was a real beauty and perfect for my dad," he said and began to pace the room. "Nobody dared say a word against her, not while Grandpa Liam was around. Behind his back was another story and then she got pregnant with Hill." He watched one hand stroking the other. "My uncles- Pitch and Aaron, they were great- been that way as long as I can remember." Jaw muscles clenched as his gaze narrowed.

"Humphrey, Vale...Gabriel- they hated all of it. Hated Hill because he was the first grandson and black- a *moulignon*. Hmph, I came to know that word well.

Then, they discovered Hill could pass for one of 'em- just a little on the dark side like my Uncle Pitch. Did you know he's not my grandmother's child?" Smoak looked over at Sabra, but didn't expect her to respond. "His mother was a black woman. She and my grandfather...." He shrugged. "Other than that, Pitch and Hill were just like them. Perfection. So was Pike..."

Smoak took one of the armchairs facing the view and studied his hands again. "There was no changing what I'd grow up looking like." He smiled then. "My parents were happy though. I've only ever known love from them.

Unconditionally," his smile deepened. "My mother's the greatest woman I know," he shrugged. "She always told me I could do anything, *be* anything. She named me Smoak after one of my grandfather Hillar's nephews but said she really did it so I'd never forget how elusive it was. She said when people see smoke; they know it has the tendency to bring destruction if not properly tended."

Sabra cleared her throat when her heart somersaulted. "Miss Imani's an insightful lady."

"Yeah…they never got to her. She was too strong for them and they knew it." Pride carried in his voice. "Dad wasn't havin' it though, he cut off all contact. They didn't even see Caiphus 'til he was six I think…my grandparents begged Dad to let them know us- all of us." He sighed.

"They were good people. I think it was a little hard for my grandmother though. She never seemed to dote on me the way she did Hill, Pike and Cai." He smiled over the shortening of his little brother's name.

"I never told my dad any of it and I really did love my grandparents almost as much as I hate my uncles." The fist clenched again, that time slamming his palm.

"Gabriel was an ass. Me and Brogue were the same age- Gabriel poured all his…crap into Brogue. He's changed a lot from those days but back then he made visiting the family sheer hell. I hated him enough to kill him."

Sabra came to kneel at his chair. "So you just lived with it?"

"Wasn't so bad," he gave her a crooked smile. "I didn't live around 'em. Didn't even spend much time around Brogue. He was Pike's shadow, but he and I didn't have anything in common." He took her hand off his knee and squeezed. "Until you."

A Lover's Hate

Tears pooled her luminous gaze and she jerked him into a hug. "I'm sorry," she closed her eyes tightly shut.

Smoak's embrace was just as tight. "Do you mind if we get the hell out of here?"

Sabra's sob mingled with laughter. "You'll have to make the call to settle up the bill."

He chuckled over her reminder about his responsibilities per restaurant rules. He took his time moving, preferring to keep his face pressed into her neck.

***

"Imani."

Frowning slightly, Imani turned her face away from the voice that was working to wake her. The voice persisted however, calling her name again. Eventually, her lashes fluttered and she realized she was in bed. She tried to turn her face into a pillow and discovered she couldn't.

Roman was preventing it. His hand covered her upper arm and his grip wasn't loose. Imani blinked herself fully awake then. Finally, she focused on her husband's handsome olive-toned face.

"What's wrong?"

He responded with a kiss. Imani participated in her usual manner until she realized Roman's kisses held an intensity that was changed from the husbandly pecks she'd grown used to. She pressed on his chest until he released her mouth.

"What's wrong?" Her dark eyes searched his for the answer.

"I'm beginning to think nothing's wrong." His words sounded sweet yet laced with an edgy undercurrent. He dipped his head, nibbling her earlobe as his fingers trailed a lazy path along the line of her thigh.

AlTonya Washington

Imani realized then that she was only covered by sheets. Her lips parted for a moan that she dared not give. In fact, she stifled any response to his touch. "Roman, what are you doing?" She asked when he raised his head.

"What does it feel like?" His free hand tightened in the lush hair framing her face and he prevented her from looking away.

"What does it feel like Imani?" His voice was soft, coaxing a reply.

His middle finger began a slow trace of her sex and then delved inside the satin folds. Imani's lashes swept her cheeks when she closed her eyes. Instantly, she rotated her hips on his touch.

"Jesus, Imani!" His words were hushed but his shock was evident as he bolted upright in the mammoth sized bed they shared.

The sound of their breathing filled the room for long moments.

"How long?" He demanded. "How long have you known you could walk?"

"Who told you?" She challenged.

"Fuck! Nobody told me! How long, Immi?"

She left the bed. "Two years." She snatched the robe from a bench at the front of the bed.

Roman came to his feet with a swiftness to rival a man half his age.

Imani read the fury in his expression and sat down in the nearest chair.

Roman bolted over and pulled her to her feet. "Uh-uh. You've done enough of that. You kept this from me for two years? Why?" his brilliant stare repeatedly roamed the length of her shapely frame. "Why?" his voice grated.

A Lover's Hate

Imani wiped at tears that wouldn't stop coming. "You said you'd kill him," she hiccupped.

Roman's expertly carved features grew more striking as they hardened. "Since when is your loyalty to my brother?"

"It's not!"

"You could've fuckin' well fooled me Imani!"

"My loyalty is to you." She clutched her hands before her chest. "You couldn't expect me to just do nothing to keep you from charging out and killing that snake."

Roman came close and set his mouth against her ear. "That's what we do," he said.

She shook her head vehemently. "Not you. You're not like that."

He stormed the room then, raking all ten fingers through the glossy thickness of his dark hair. "If I had been like that, maybe they wouldn't have thought they could try this shit and get away with it." Again, he studied her from head to toe and then cursed and rolled his eyes.

"How did you know?" She asked. He took so long to answer; she thought he may not have heard her quietly spoken question.

"I've suspected for months." His face softened a little when he saw that he had stunned her. "Do you realize how well I know you?" he moved close to her again. "Do you understand how well I read your kisses?" He brushed his thumb across her mouth. "I know when you kiss me to get me to shut up. When you think I've done something sweet, when you're proud of me, when you want me…" he closed his hand over her neck and nuzzled his nose with hers. "I always know when you want me," He moved back to look at her.

"I'd lost track until I was talking to Pike-he was telling me how he knew Sabella still loved him and asking if I didn't *just know* that you loved me without question."

He shook his head then. "I've been so worried for you, wracked with guilt over you being in that blasted chair when it should've been me and all this time you..." he distanced himself from her then. Passing a heavy armchair, he turned it on its side with little more than a flick of his wrist.

Imani could only watch him, his back turned as he took in heavy breaths. Taking courage in both hands, she went to him.

"Roman?"

"Not now, Immi."

Boldly, she trailed her fingertips across the copper colored, sweat-slicked skin of his back. "Would you rather spend the night angry with me or taking what I've denied you for two years?" Exercising more boldness, she sealed the distance between them and put a tentative kiss between his shoulder blades. She kept her lips there until he turned.

His kiss was almost brutal at first and then it infused with desire, longing and remembrance. He helped himself to her as though he were starved which, of course, he was. When he stopped; looking as though he were uncertain, Imani let her robe fall to the floor.

"You don't have to be careful," she reassured and moved back toward the bed.

***

Seattle, Washington~

"I gotta make a move, Twig." Moses Ramsey groaned, though not in a way that sounded painful.

A Lover's Hate

"So go ahead," Johari made no effort to disentangle herself from her husband.

They lay wrapped in each other's arms after a heated romp that started in the foyer; following their return from a jazz show and ended in their bedroom. Johari snuggled in closer and grazed her lips along Moses' jaw, and then she had the nerve to sigh contently.

"I really do have to get up. Got some calls to make. Check in with some of the guys on assignment."

"'Kay," Johari yawned, smiling as she snuggled in more content. To make matters 'worse', she rubbed her thumbnail across Moses' nipple and smiled when he gave her hand a warning clutch.

"Your lack of respect for my business is disturbing." He said, deep voice lazy, eyes still closed.

"Then let me make up for it." She inched up to nibble his ear.

"Damn you," Moses grunted and flipped Jo to her back. He followed the action with a deep kiss.

The couple was in the midst of resuming earlier activities when the phone rang.

"No..."

"I'm sorry."

"Can't they leave a message?" She began to rub herself enticingly against him.

"I swear I'll make it up to you."

"Repeatedly and enthusiastically?"

"Of course," he frowned humorously. "Who do you think you're talkin' to?"

"Hmph," Jo pretended to be unconvinced, but decided to let him handle his call. She received a slap to her bare ass as she crawled from the king bed.

AlTonya Washington

Moses shook his head while taking in the deliberate show she made of sauntering from the room. He leaned over to grab the cordless from its mount and grinned at the sound of Carlos McPhereson's voice.

"Not in the mood to talk to the voice mail, huh?" He asked his old friend.

"Gram Walters is dead, Mo."

Moses pushed up to sit. "You're sure?"

"Very."

"How'd you find out?"

"News is late. They think he may've been dead a couple of weeks before they found him. His throat was cut."

Moses left the bed. "I'm guessing the cops have no leads." He stroked his jaw while he paced.

"They've got a note." Carlos said.

Moses waited.

"'For your attention, E.'"

FIFTEEN

"I thought we were going to my- *your* villa?" Sabra was asking when the elevator bumped to a stop at her penthouse. They had left the restaurant where two unfinished drinks rounded out their order.

"*I'm* going back." Smoak clarified.

"Why?"

He didn't answer and Sabra let the silence carry until they'd covered the wing leading to her door. It didn't occur to her, until that moment, what a very long day it had been. Still, she was in no mood to be alone and knew the loneliness would do Smoak no good either.

"Will you stay?" She asked, curling her fingers against his chest and letting him hear the need in her voice.

"I can't," he wouldn't look at her.

"Why?"

"Not a good idea."

"Why?"

A Lover's Hate

"Dammit Sabra, just let me go alright?" His whisper was harsh, impatient.

She only shook her head. "I know it wasn't easy telling me what you did and I know telling me hasn't made you forget it."

"So let me leave then."

"No," she bumped her fists against his chest, "let's go to the villa like you wanted."

He sighed. "It's not a good time."

"I think it's a fine time. You shouldn't be alone."

He grinned but the gesture held hardness and no humor. "Are you serious?" The words came out as a hiss.

She nodded and he took the key from her hand. He unlocked the door and stepped insofar as to toss the key to a table just inside the door.

"Goodnight," he called over his shoulder.

"Maybe if you'd shared some part of your childhood with me back then I-"

He slammed the door and turned on her, effectively stifling the words she blurted. Approaching her again, he tilted her chin up.

"Are you going to tell me you wouldn't have fucked my cousin had you known?" he looked as though he regretted the words the second he heard them. "Let me go, Sabe."

But she was desperate to make him stay. Blinded by need and some insane desire, she yearned for him to use her to vent the considerable anger he was fighting to hide. Grasping the lapels of the tailored oatmeal colored suit jacket, she pulled him into a throaty kiss.

Smoak gave in naturally, hungrily thrusting his tongue against hers. His loss of control didn't last long and he set her away.

AlTonya Washington

Sabra shivered on the sensation coursing through her. Powerful hands bit into her flesh where he gripped her bare upper arms.

"Let me leave," he spoke the words slowly, firmly as though that delivery would help her to understand.

Instead, Sabra moved forward until he was against the wall. Ravenously, she nipped and grazed her teeth across his collarbone. Smoak was undoubtedly aroused, almost always a given in her presence. It was surely a definite reaction when she was pressed next to him and whispering into his skin- begging him to fuck her.

Arousal nudging against anger was a dangerous thing. It was dangerous for her-dangerous to provoke him. She knew him too well not to sense the rage inside. She'd always known there was animosity between him and Brogue. Why the hell did she need him to go into the particulars of it? He wondered.

Sabra was still nibbling his collarbone. She was focused on getting him out of the jacket and shirt he wore. All the while, she murmured words of need into his chest.

"Sabra," he wrenched her away and gave her a few good shakes. "What the fuck are you doing? You of all people should know better than to test me. Or have you forgotten?" He shook her again. "I could have killed you that day."

"But you didn't. You didn't do that…" Lashes moving like hummingbird wings, she appeared to be swooning on the memory of what he *did* do.

Smoak had all but lost his grip on restraint. He bowed his head and let his eyes drift shut in an attempt to ward off the combination of fury and desire that rose like a storm inside him. When he opened his eyes and saw the sly element lurking in her toffee gaze; while a knowing smile curved her generous mouth, it finished him.

He slammed her against the wall. Sabra gasped amidst his stoked temper, but somehow she appeared content. Expectancy had her heart racing when he cuffed his hand about her throat. He squeezed, bringing his dark beautiful face within mere inches hers.

"You know what I'm capable of and I could swear you want more of it."

Wickedly, her lashes lilted, her smile broadened. "Your cousin was very...eager that day. Whatever fantasies he had, he fulfilled them." She grunted when his hand tightened anew on her throat. His free hand disappeared beneath the scalloped hem of her dress.

She weakened. "That's it..."

Anger peaked, Smoak made quick work of her underwear, ripping it badly when he groped at the lace hugging her hips and ample derriere. She moved to touch him, to help him out of his shirt but he wanted none of those niceties. He released her throat to take her wrists and kept them pressed above her head against the wall.

Sabra could have laughed she was so pleasured by the sheer anticipation of getting what she'd craved for so long. Their time together over the last few days had been beyond exquisite, but *this* was what she wanted. Just like this...

Smoak was driving his tongue inside her ear. His hand on her wrists was bruise-inducing. The fabric of torn panties hung in shreds around her lush thighs but not for long. He muttered something profane and proceeded to jerk the material free. Resting his face in the crook of her neck, he buried his fingers inside her. He heard her laughter then; it held the sound of complete elation.

AlTonya Washington

Her hair was in disarray, covering her face in a tangle of curls. Sabra found his ear through the tousle of her hair and she outlined its shape with the tip of her tongue.

Smoak angled away from her intimate exploration. He hooked a hand about her thigh and brought it alongside his hip while he undid his pants and freed himself. He penetrated her fast. His sex was fully extended; its considerable build filled her in a wild melding of pleasure and pain. Displaying an enviable albeit understated show of finesse, he kept her wrists shackled above her head and took her with no intention to show mercy.

Sabra barely realized it when he finally released her hands. They remained positioned as they'd been until her brain registered the freedom. Lack of strength in the limbs, sent them slipping down past her head. Smoak kept her thighs secured high at his hips before easily slipping his hands beneath her ass, cradling it for thrusts that elicited the telltale moisture-rich sounds of need along with Sabra's gasping cries and the ragged groans from deep within his chest.

The framed landscaped pictures clattered just slightly against the walls, but the lovers didn't notice. Sabra hung her arms over Smoak's broad shoulders. She was tentatively testing his willingness to let her touch him.

He offered no resistance, so she raked her nails across the silky strands of jet hair crowning his head. She wanted him to kiss her. Her tongue ached to do battle with his, but this wasn't that type of scene. Tender acts of kissing and caressing had no place among the frenzied, rough slams of his sex inside hers.

His deep groans began to resemble animalistic growls that stroked her passion as fully as his hands flexing on her body as he ravished her. She shrieked once from the pain when his grip became unbearable. He came hard. The rush of it pounded into her like a flood.

Sabra brushed her nose against his temple and cheek to absorb his cologne and the purely male essence beneath it. Slowly, she clenched her inner walls about his shaft still rigid despite its eruption.

Smoak dragged Sabra with him to the floor and slapped at her hands when she would have pulled him out of his shirt. He treated her dress to the same fate her panties had met earlier. She brought a fist down hard on his thigh cursing his disregard for her things and emitting a little fire beneath the submissive display she'd given seconds before.

Smoak punished her with the kiss she'd begged for. It was as relentlessly demanding as his earlier drives inside her core. Sabra moaned, unable to breathe beneath the force of his tongue down her throat. She swallowed around it and reciprocated with a similar show of strength in her own kiss.

Smoak ended the gesture and rose above her again. He showed about as much regard for his own clothes as he had for hers. Still, he managed not to rip any of the finely crafted garments as he pulled them from a toned, flawlessly chiseled physique. Sabra trembled and began a slow grind into the floor as she pleasured herself to the sight of him.

Pushing her hands aside, Smoak replaced them with his mouth. Sabra's lips parted to emit a moan but there was no sound. Delight had its way with her as she flexed her walls about his filling tongue.

Smoak shed what remained of his clothes then. Tasting himself inside her body lengthened his dick as renewed desire firmed it. Sabra was raking her nails over his head, luxuriating in the satiny texture brushing her palms. Meanwhile, Smoak alternated between drinking deeply of her and showering her thighs with kisses.

Lacing his fingers through hers, he pressed them to the floor next to her rotating hips. Moments later, he was inside her again and filling her more potently than his tongue ever could. He nestled his face in the valley between her heavy breasts and settled the full force of his weight against her.

Sabra relished it, curving her hands about his taut ass squeezing as it flexed when he entered and withdrew from her. He withdrew fully before he came again and pulled her up to sit when she reached to urge him back down.

Sabra tried unintelligibly to question his intentions and found herself bent over the back of a nearby chair. He kicked apart her feet still encased in the spiked-heel sandals that complimented the mallard blue of her dress. She could have dissolved into the cushions of the big chair. The feel of him from behind, probing her there, sent a shiver throughout her body. He used one hand to fondle her labia, then his index, ring and middle fingers disappeared inside her. He subjected her to an obscene fingering that followed every withdrawal of his erection from her drenched and well-used sex.

His other hand was hidden in the tumbled mass of her hair. He wound a hoard of thick curls around his fist and positioned Sabra to his satisfaction. When she tried to straighten or lower more than he wanted, he simply tightened his grip on her hair.

Sabra could hardly curve her fingers into the chair cushions. Every part of her felt weak, depleted. She'd lost count of the orgasms and her inner thighs were sticky with the rich coating of need that had oozed during their sexual

A Lover's Hate

event. Only one of her sexy sandals remained and Smoak seemed intent on taking her out of it with his vigorous thrusts.

He kept his grip tight in her hair; his fingers went deep rotating inside her as he leaned over her back to let his sensuously sculpted lips graze the alluring dip of her spine.

"Smoak please…" she didn't know if she begged him to go on or to stop.

Smoak guessed it was the latter. "Take it," he said as his mouth moved up over her shoulder toward her cheek.

He came raggedly, breathing heavily into her hair as shudders wracked his muscular build. He kept Sabra bent to his will until he was spent inside her. He withdrew after a while and directed her around to the front of the chair.

"Just a little nap…" she pleaded in earnest then.

He smiled and dropped into the chair, pulling her down with him. She was asleep on his lap in less than two minutes.

No such luck for him. He inhaled the faint freshness of her damp hair and dropped kisses to her temple. The smile remained as he reached down to pull off the sandal barely clinging to her foot then. In one seamless move, he stood with her in his arms and headed toward her bedroom.

Soft lighting triggered by electronic timer, bathed the room. As though she weighed less than an ounce, Smoak situated Sabra across his shoulder and turned down her bed. He tucked her into the covers and then sat to watch her.

He wanted to stay with her, but knew that he wouldn't. The memories stirred by their earlier chat had found a less invasive place to reside but they had returned to the front of his thoughts. The anger they conjured, he had somehow forgotten while he was with her.

AlTonya Washington

Looking down on Sabra as she slept, he realized it was nothing new. She'd always had the power to silence his demons. She'd done it so subtly, he hadn't been aware. Her strength, hell her stubbornness had saved him. She settled him, kept him lucid when the need for vengeance would've had him flying off the deep end and dipping his hand into all manner of idiocy.

He smoothed a hand over her cheek, then kissed her there and prepared to go. He stood to draw the covers up around her neck, then frowned and leaned closer. His head tilted at a curious angle as he focused on a flicker of light near the bedpost.

He looked toward the post nearest him and noticed the same flickering. Slowly, he pulled back the bed covers and moved closer to ensure that his eyes weren't deceiving him.

Reaching out, he took hold of the chain dangling from the post. Even as he held onto the glimmering links of metal, uncertainty shimmered in his midnight stare. His fingers trailed the length of the chain down to the fur-lined cuffs at the end.

"What the fuck?" he whispered.

SIXTEEN

"He said...he said he would hurt you and daddy if I told. Did he-? Did he take Aiesha with him? I think she wanted to go. I mean I-she seemed like she liked him. He was doing stuff...and she was laughing and then she saw me and- he said he would hurt you and daddy and then he left-"

Sabra flinched awake. Her eyes were wide, breathing rapid as she scanned her bedroom. Smoak was gone, but he had been there. What had happened there last night was as real as what happened in the dream she'd just had.

So where was Smoak? How had she wound up in bed? Did he put her there? Did he see-

Loud voices in the corridor signaled the arrival of Lee Lee and Sabra's stylist Cheryl Hess. Sabra removed

her displaced look and put on a less revealing one for Lee Lee who was telling Cheryl to go on and set up in the salon.

"Alright Cher, we'll be out in a second! Hey girl," Lee Lee greeted Sabra brightly when she arrived in the bedroom. "Cher's out here for your appointment and not a bit too soon I see-uggh…" Lee took in her friend's disheveled appearance.

"At least you look like you got some good sleep. Cher's gonna kill you for not wrapping your hair." Lee patted her bouncy bob for emphasis.

"Alright then, just gimme a second." Sabra pushed at the bed covers.

"Well make it quick," Lee passed a chair and grabbed Sabra's dress from the previous day. "We've got a full day- the appointment with Cheryl's doubling as a meeting for the hair show and then we're meeting with Smoak and his people."

"Smoak?" Sabra watched Lee shove her dress and underthings into a hamper.

"The architects for his lab compound," Lee's voice was muffled from the depths of the wardrobe room. "They want to discuss things with the resort architects."

"Do I have to be there?" Sabra asked when Lee emerged from the closet.

"Well," Lee frowned briefly debating, "it'd look strange if you weren't 'specially at this early stage, you know?"

Sabra only nodded her agreement, but jumped when Lee clapped and told her to get a move on.

"Me and Cher are over in the salon. We'll have coffee and stuff waiting." Lee walked over to tug a lock of Sabra's hair and then she nodded toward one of the cuffs dangling from the bedpost.

"Have you needed them yet?"

"No." Sabra worked up a smile.

"See? Told you, you were overreacting," Lee tugged Sabra's hair again. "Hurry up," she ordered and then left the room.

***

Paris, France~

Contessa Warren Ramsey was rubbing sleep from her eyes and allowing her nose to lead her out toward the scent of coffee and other breakfast delights.

"Our very own I-HOP," she yawned upon finding her husband in the tiny dining alcove nestled between the kitchen and living area of the spacious suite. Their awe-inspiring hotel resided in one of the city's most exclusive districts.

Fernando set a box of croissants to the table before the windows. "Price you pay for sleeping all afternoon," he jibed.

County yawned again. "It's a price I'd *gladly* pay," her eyes sparkled playfully then. "And let us not forget Ramsey *why* I had to sleep all afternoon."

Fernando's striking, crystalline gaze narrowed and he met his wife halfway to the table. There, he reached beneath his shirt which was; at that moment, smothering County's body. Cradling her bare tush in his big hands, he squeezed.

"So I *made* you do it, huh?"

Contessa felt herself instantly reacting to his touch. "I can recall asking- no *begging* for a nap after our *bath* this morning."

Fernando's grin triggered the adorable crinkles at the corners of his light eyes as he recalled their long morning. *Bathing* had been the very last thing on their agenda.

Fernando rested his face in the side of Contessa's neck and breathed in the mingling of their scents on her skin.

"Least I can do is make up for treating you so shamefully," he said.

County stood on her toes to rub herself against him while her fingers splayed across his wide honey-toned chest.

"Making up's fine as long as you promise to treat me shamefully again later."

Hoisting her high, Fernando carted her off toward the alcove. "That's a promise I'll be happy to keep."

***

Cheryl Hess was putting the finishing touches on the style for her most demanding customer. The fact that Sabra Ramsey was one of her biggest clients didn't give Cheryl any qualms about voicing her considerable opinions about the way the woman took care of her hair.

"You've got too much of this mess not to have it relaxed." Cheryl balked and used a stylish clip to sweep a group of curls away from Sabra's face.

"Natural hair is healthy hair. Isn't that what folks are always saying? You tryin' to tell me that's not true, Cher?"

"Bitch," Cheryl sighed the phrase. She brushed the tip of one curl before letting it bounce across Sabra's shoulder.

"Hell yeah, it's true but running a hot comb through this shit is a mutha. I would *not* be offended if you went elsewhere to have it pressed."

AlTonya Washington

Laughter erupted among the three women in the private salon Sabra had constructed inside her penthouse apartment. The dwelling was state of the art, complete with spa facilities equipped for massages, manicures, pedicures and facials. Despite her opinions on pressing Sabra Ramsey's long, thick hair, Cheryl considered house calls to the exquisite domain well worth her time.

The appointment was a working one for Lee Lee who had jotted down notes while the entrepreneurs went back and forth on ideas about the hair show. She had taken a wealth of notes that would get them started. At that moment, Lee Lee was trying to choose a new nail polish from the array of colors that filled a far wall.

Smoak had arrived at the apartment just as Sabra and Cheryl resumed their debate about her hair. He halted his progress toward the salon when he heard Sabra's laughter and he smiled at the sound. Leaning against the corridor wall, he stroked the back of his hand across his jaw and debated. He wanted to go back to her room for another look at the chains on the bed.

She had company, so he decided against it. Then, he reasoned that the restraints could be about nothing. He knew better than that though.

The women's voices got his attention again and he continued his trek toward the salon.

Lee Lee had selected a nail color she was on the fence about. It happened to be the one Sabra was sporting and she told Lee Lee to come take a look.

"I know this color is better on delicious maple syrup complexions like mine," Sabra drawled when Lee took her hand to observe, "but you could probably make it work with that yellow skin."

A Lover's Hate

Laughter rang out again as Smoak crossed the foyer outside the salon. He preferred to observe the women unaware. His pitch stare was locked on Lee Lee's hand holding with Sabra. He wondered then whether their familiar behavior was about more than being best friends. Before last night, he'd have said 'no way'.

Sabra Ramsey was a male magnet if such a thing could exist. She'd had that power since he'd known her and he knew it was a power she relished. Maybe the chains were props for men lucky enough to spend time in her bed. Possible, but the thought sent a rumble of displeasure through his chest.

Cheryl was belting out another contagious barrel of laughter when she noticed the very tall intense looking male in the salon doorway. Her laughter hitched on an awkward sound of appreciation.

Lee Lee caught the direction of Cheryl's gaze and turned to follow it. Sabra had seen Smoak there shortly after her stylist gasped. When Cheryl uttered a breathless 'yes sir?', Sabra left the chair knowing the appointment was over. If there was one thing Cheryl Hess would drop everything for, it was the chance to introduce herself to a god.

Smoak's charm was at its coveted level of potency when he approached Cheryl with an outstretched hand.

"I should've known she had help lookin' so damn good," he nodded toward Sabra once he and Cheryl exchanged pleasantries.

Sabra acknowledged the compliment with a faint smile when she met his gaze.

"Well you certainly don't need any help looking good; exactly what *do* you need help with?" Cheryl's dark eyes sparkled with a naughty fire. She possessed her own caliber of charm and had Smoak grinning bashfully in seconds.

"I'm actually here to see Sabra, if she's got a minute," Smoak announced once the largest portion of his laughter was spent.

Lee Lee knew Cheryl wouldn't relinquish her moment with Smoak anytime soon so she took it upon herself to casually escort the woman from the salon.

"Are you alright?" Smoak queried once he and Sabra were alone. The easy charm in his eyes was replaced by something more searching.

"I'm good," Sabra turned her back and made a show of straightening pins and combs along the counter. Her movements stilled when she heard the soft rustle of his jeans as he walked up behind her. She allowed another few seconds to pass and then turned. Moving to her toes, she brushed a dutiful kiss across his jaw.

Smoak reciprocated by squeezing her arms and watched her wince at the bruises he knew he had put there. "You're good. That's the truth?" He released her arms.

"Please don't apologize for anything. I wanted it." She tried to step around him but he blocked the move.

"Not that we need a reason to argue but you picked that fight with me on purpose, didn't you?"

"We didn't fight."

"Just what the fuck would you call it, Sabe?"

She bowed her head. "Why did you leave last night?"

"What makes you think I left?"

"I woke up- you weren't here."

He toyed with a curl clinging to the rise of her breast visible above a fitted pink scoop-necked T-shirt. "Do you remember falling asleep in my lap?"

Sabra bit her lip on the memory. Of course she remembered. "I woke up in bed," she said. She risked a look at him then and her heart flipped in reply to the crooked smile he flashed.

"Well then," he sighed, appearing content with where things stood on the matter.

"Did you put me there?"

"Sabra…do you honestly think I'd put you to bed and leave you there alone?"

The idea struck her as ridiculous as well. She shook her head once.

"Are you having trouble remembering how you got there?" Any trace of humor was removed from his face and voice. He saw that she couldn't answer and took pity. Cupping her cheek, he held her in place for a kiss.

She whimpered, ready for him. As though she hadn't been kissed in weeks; her tongue hungrily pursued his. Bravely, she rubbed her chest against his until she succeeded in baring one breast above the scooping bodice of the T-shirt.

"Put me in your mouth," she ordered and he obeyed. She melted on the sensation but managed to go to work undoing the jeans fastening that was covered by the hem of the clay colored shirt he wore. She was so absorbed in grinding her hips against his that she had some trouble working the jean clasp free.

Smoak braced his hands to the counter behind Sabra. Her whimpering into his neck and rubbing against his dick had him aroused and ready to take her out of the flimsy shorts she wore.

"Hell," he growled when the piercing ring of his cell phone filled the air.

"Ignore it," she said.

"Every intention of it," he promised. His face was half hidden in her top. One hand was inside her shorts, clutching her ass.

Sabra roped her arms about his neck and she kissed him tentatively. He didn't resist the gesture and she carefully added her tongue to the mix.

He tired of the uncertain teasing and ravenously claimed her mouth. The phone began to ring again.

"Let it go. You won't be sorry."

"Counting on it," he groaned into her neck, but pulled the phone from his pocket to check the faceplate. Curious, he turned his back to Sabra and pushed to redial the missed call from his cousin.

Sabra fixed her clothes and watched him on the phone. When he clicked off the device, confusion shadowed his face.

In one fluid move, he turned, closed the brief distance to Sabra and kissed her hard.

"I have to go," he said and did so without another word.

SEVENTEEN

Smoak's single knock to the door was answered by Roman. Surprised silent, Smoak tracked his father's footsteps through the foyer of the high rollers' chalet and into the living room where Brogue Tesano sat in an armchair near the fireplace. Crimson blushed the eggshell shirt he wore. His throat had been opened from ear to ear.

"Son of a bitch," Smoak breathed, his surprise mixing with disbelief. He looked to his father unable to speak the question apparent in his black eyes.

"I came to talk about Gabriel," Roman shrugged. "I found him here like that- called Pitch," he frowned at his son then. "What are you doing here?"

"Brogue just called me."

"When?" Pitch asked, moving away from his place near the mantle.

"Just now, a little over ten minutes ago. I saw his name on the faceplate, but when I dialed back, he picked up but didn't say anything."

Roman and Pitch shared meaningful looks. Pitch pulled a handkerchief from an inside pocket of his suede butter cream jacket. He felt across Brogue's pockets and used the handkerchief to retrieve a phone.

"Not possible," Pitch murmured in disbelief. The phone showed a dialed call fourteen minutes prior.

"He's been dead for hours," Roman noted.

Smoak could see that judging from his cousin's pallor, the congealed blood on the floor and the dried state of it on the man's skin and clothes. "Who did this?" he asked.

There were no guesses.

"So what now?" Smoak asked the men.

"We get him out of here." Pitch told his nephew. "Grekka will scream bloody hell, and with all of us here in the same hotel… wouldn't look good."

"This kind of attention wouldn't be good for Sabra either."

Smoak blinked at the sound of her name. Quietly, he acknowledged the logic in his father's words. "Can I do anything?" He asked.

"You shouldn't even be here." Roman's tone was sharp.

"Go to your girl and don't let her out of your sight," Pitch interjected. "And for God's sake keep her away from this room 'til we've gone over it."

"The cleaning crew is like clockwork." Smoak worked his hands across the muscles bunched tight at the back of his neck. "They're obsessive about keeping things pristine around here."

"We'll handle 'em." Pitch said.

"Did um…whoever did this, did they leave anything behind- a lead we can follow up on?" Smoak noticed another meaningful glance shift between his father and uncle.

"Christ, Dad come on," Smoak's voice was low and laced with agitation.

Roman nodded toward Pitch who produced a maroon stained scrap of paper. The item was secured between two glass coasters from the bar in the room.

"In the slit where his throat was cut," Pitch explained.

Smoak angled the note and scanned it once before reciting. "For your attention, E."

Roman shrugged. "We don't know. But we'll find out."

"Now *you* get the hell out of here." Pitch directed.

Smoak scanned the room once more and then did as he was told.

***

"Mommy?" Sabra used her key to let herself into Georgia's villa later that morning. The dream/memory from the night before was still nibbling away at her sanity. She needed to talk and her mother was the only one who knew that subject matter.

The villa was dim as Georgia tended to keep it when she slept. Sabra checked her watch; her mother was usually up shopping or having a spa treatment by 9am when she spent time at the resort. To find her still slumbering past 11am was very out of character.

Sabra took the stairway to the bedroom that spanned the entire second floor.

A Lover's Hate

"Mommy?" She called, dropping a knock to the tall red oak door.

There was a thud on the other side of the door. Sabra walked in to find her mother retrieving the bottle of her favorite Russian Vodka from the floor.

"Everything okay?"

Georgia laughed at her daughter's question. "I'm such a klutz. Good thing the cap was on." She gave the bottle a perfunctory shake. "What are you doing here, sweetie?"

"We need to talk." Sabra folded her arms over the blouse styled bodice of the clover dress she sported.

"Ah baby…" Georgia inched up in the bed. "I had such a late night at the tables. Can it wait 'til after I shower and make myself gorgeous?"

Sabra shook her head and smiled. Georgia Ramsey could spend a day ditch digging and still look ready to walk a runway.

"Make it fast, Mommy. This is important."

"Okay baby, I'll-"

A flushing sound halted more speaking. Sabra's eyes moved toward the bathroom door. Her brows lifted a notch when she looked toward her mother. The woman appeared to be in no hurry to explain.

Patiently, Sabra waited sliding her hands over the fine, clinging fabric of her dress. The door opened and Felix Cade's tall, still athletic frame filled the space. He leaned against the jamb and set his hand against the door.

"Sorry Georgie," he winked in his ex-wife's direction and then sent one to his daughter. "Mornin' Babygirl."

"Daddy?" Sabra told herself to close her mouth, but she couldn't. "A late night at the tables," she repeated her mother's excuse, "*At* the tables or *on* one?"

"Honey-"

"You two hate each other!"

Georgia moved uncomfortably near the head board. "You can hate someone and still have sex with them."

Sabra covered her face. "Good grief," she groaned.

"We don't really hate each other," Felix clarified, "Babygirl we just can't ever seem to agree."

Silence settled among the family until Felix made a play at checking his watch which hung off the nightstand near the tangled bed.

"Ah damn, I need to head on up out of here."

"Don't even try it," Georgia snapped. "You're not leavin' me here to explain this."

"Ah babe," Felix grabbed his shirt, still twisted in the covers, "you're who she came to see anyway," he eased a Rolex over his wrist and snapped the timepiece in place. Leaning across the bed, he dropped a kiss to Georgia's mouth.

"I'll see you later," he murmured during the kiss.

Georgia was definitely smiling when Felix pulled away. Sabra felt a smile pressuring her mouth as well. She savored the tiny sprig of happiness planted by her parents of all people.

"I'll see you later, sugar." Felix was pulling his daughter into a tight squeeze and kissing her forehead.

"So how long has this been going on?" Sabra asked her mother when they were alone.

"Off and on for years," Georgia kept her eyes on the bed covers. "But we haven't been together like this for a long time- not until Fernando's wedding."

A Lover's Hate

Then, in a purely girlish un-Georgia Ramsey fashion, she pressed the sheet to her face and giggled.

"Oh honey, don't give me a hard time about this," Georgia begged.

"I wouldn't dream of it. Looks like Daddy's given you a hard time already."

Laughter rang out wildly between mother and daughter then.

"So can we have our talk now?"

"Sure, baby."

Sabra went to make coffee while Georgia made herself presentable.

"Please don't tell me to forget about it and it'll go away-that doesn't work anymore. I'm not sure it ever did."

"It's my fault," Georgia rested her elbows on her knees and dropped her face into her hands.

Sabra scooted across the sofa to rub Georgia's shoulders. "Don't Mommy."

"No Sabra. I smothered you, I know I did and still do. I smothered you in hopes of smothering out the vileness of what you saw that night and at such a young impressionable age."

"It wasn't your fault. It was his."

Georgia shook her head. "I should have taken you to see someone."

"And tell 'em what, Ma? That I witnessed Gabriel Tesano having rough sex with my seventeen year old babysitter, that she seemed to be into it or that the creep threatened to do the same to me, you *and* daddy if I ever told anyone?" Sabra's expression reflected hopelessness. "No one could have helped me with a story like that."

"Baby…" Georgia pushed a curl back from Sabra's face. "You've suffered so much because of it."

"No more than most." Sabra took her mother's hand and squeezed it. "Did you know he was responsible for Imani Tesano's accident?"

Again, Georgia leaned forward on the sofa and covered her face with her hands. "I'd heard rumors of it- heard your uncles talking about it…but I was never interested in hearing much else about that swine after what you told me."

"Smoak suspects- he doesn't know it's anything like this," Sabra quickly explained when Georgia's eyes filled with questions. "He knows there's something…not right with me and he knows it goes back a long way.

I can't hide it Mommy," she flopped back on the sofa. "I'm no good at pretending around him."

Georgia smiled. "You still love him."

"I want to give myself over to him." Sabra massaged her temples. "I want him to handle it- handle me." She spoke with some hesitation then.

"And you think I don't understand that?" Georgia fanned out her black gauzy robe and crossed her legs beneath it.

"Hmph," Sabra fixed her mother with a skeptical look. "Who could, Mommy? Belle and Bill looked at me like I'd lost my mind when I told them about my *submissive tendencies*."

"Did you tell them about Gabriel?"

Sabra shook her head. "Only about what I was going through and that I…enjoyed the way Smoak treated me that day he found me…with Brogue. Mama how am I supposed to tell Smoak that- bring that into our bed?"

"Because that's where it belongs especially with the man you love." Georgia slammed her fists to the sofa. "You were dealt a shitty hand of cards but this is a part of who you are. Smoak deserves to know about it."

Sabra left the sofa, the heels of her cream pumps disappeared into the deep black carpeting. "What's he gonna think of me, Mama?"

"That you're strong and capable."

"I'm sick of being strong."

"Because it's not easy," Georgia smiled understandingly. "But even a strong woman finds fulfillment at times in relinquishing some of that power. We might, *ignore* those needs- daydream about them, just harmless fantasies after all...but it's different for you." Her elegant features hardened then.

"Ignoring them affects you- your behavior and makes you do things that could get you hurt. I've handled this very badly with you. I let fear keep me from doing what was best for my child and you've paid for it, but you've been very lucky so far, you know that?"

Sabra felt her back stiffen, but she acknowledged the truth in her mother's words. Her actions over the years could have had such different outcomes.

"Share this with him, baby. My guess is he isn't just here over some drama with the land. That sexy thing wants you back and he definitely looks to be up to the challenge of handling whatever you bring to him."

Sabra went back to the sofa where she fell into Georgia's waiting embrace.

***

After the talk with Georgia, Sabra continued her daily routine. The chat and the discovery of her parent's 'closeness' had done wonders for her mood. If only she

AlTonya Washington

could find a way to transform that into enough courage to make Smoak Tesano her most trusted confidant.

The security wing spanned the entire basement level of the first tower. There was a satellite office of equal space in the same location of the second scraper. It sounded clichéd to say the department ran like a well-oiled machine but…it did.

Sabra considered the staff and; state of the art facility she'd put in place there, to be one of her most commendable acts as owner of her vast casino resort. It was less like work and more like leisure time spent chatting with the all-male staff and its leader Franklin Robby.

Sabra and Frank were discussing the guests' questionable fashion choices while they observed footage from the cameras near the slots.

"I've got nothin' against a good bustier but that one needs to be a few sizes bigger." Sabra noted of the guest being critiqued.

"Hush up," Frank noted while stroking his goatee.

"What? Somethin' could pop out easy."

"That's what we're hopin' for…" Second in charge Owen Burke sighed as he leaned over Sabra's shoulder and studied the monitor.

The threesome had moved on to observing another guest by the time Smoak arrived. Frank and Owen were quick to greet him, recognizing Smoak's name when he introduced himself.

Smoak's easy manner and overall appreciation for the security team's stature quickly won over the men. Sabra remained perched on her spot along the observation panel. She waited for him to tell her what he was doing there.

A Lover's Hate

Smoak, it seemed, had come specifically to visit the security team.

She frowned, growing more curious when Smoak asked about cameras along the high rollers wing. Owen was happy to lay out their extensive monitoring efforts and boasted over the security provided for their guests.

"Is it possible to see footage from the night before along that area?" Smoak was asking.

Sabra abandoned her perch then. She thought better of questioning Smoak though when he gave her a look that commanded quiet.

Frank and Owen didn't question the request of course. Owen handled the task of locating the specific time frame from the private monitor where he, Frank and Sabra had been evaluating guest attire.

"Here we are. Any particular segment you're interested in Mr. Tesano?"

"Thanks Owen," Smoak moved close to observe the monitor. "High Rollers' Chalet- 882."

Sabra felt her brows tug when her frown deepened. She recognized Smoak's request as the sector where Brogue stayed whenever he visited. She maintained her quiet, waiting to see what Smoak was after.

Owen sped up the footage. The corridors were like virtual ghost towns at that time of morning. Guests were either out entertaining themselves or had already passed out into bed. There appeared to be nothing to see until the cameras captured a lone figure on the hall just after 5am.

"Can you sharpen that a little Owen?" Smoak asked.

Owen chuckled, his long reddish brows rising. "I can do better than a little," he boasted.

AlTonya Washington

Seconds later, Owen had pulled a crisp view of a woman's face.

Smoak tilted his head slightly as he worked to recall where he'd seen her. "Is she a guest or staff?" he called over his shoulder.

"We can find out." Frank turned to a row of keyboards next to where Owen worked. "I'll send the image through our facial recognition software." Frank typed in the data, then relaxed in the swivel chair before the keyboards.

"The software will cross reference the image with our staff and guest databases," Frank explained.

Sabra moved closer to Frank. "Everyone carries a key card that serves as a photo ID, room key and charge card for anything they want billed to their room and subsequently the credit card they have on file with us," she said.

"Here we go folks," Owen called. "Looks like she's one of ours. Works for the mezzanine bar. Rain Su."

"Right," Smoak nodded.

Brogue's Asian waitress.

EIGHTEEN

"Are you gonna tell me what's goin' on now?"

Sabra was past frustrated and furious. Smoak had hauled her off with him once he got the information he needed from security. They went up to the villa where Sabra had the chance to meet more members of Smoak's lab crew and special staff.

The group had made the floor their own. Apparatus of all shapes and sizes had been carted up to Sabra's main office area. She barely recognized the space. It had been completely rearranged to accommodate the needs of Smoak and his people.

They were a likable sort. Sabra made sure they knew who to contact for all their needs. Unfortunately, her easy mood with the group of scientists, analysts and engineers didn't translate over to their boss.

A Lover's Hate

One look from Smoak however, told Sabra to stifle it in the presence of his staff and she had no intention of airing dirty laundry among them. She waited until they were back at the second tower penthouse but when she walked past the foyer everything she wanted to say, vanished.

"What the hell is this?" she blasted noticing the six piece black leather luggage set in her living room.

Smoak went for the cases as though he hadn't noticed Sabra's reaction. "Good," he hefted the luggage straps over his shoulders.

"Smoak," she spread her hands when he turned on her wearing a most innocent expression. "What the fuck?" she demanded.

"Don't worry, Sweet. I don't expect you to make room in your closet." He glanced across his shoulder. "I'll just take one of the guest rooms."

"What are you doing?" She was on the verge of screaming the words.

He stopped and appeared to be seeing that she was furious for the first time. "What does it look like I'm doing?"

"Don't be an ass. I know what it looks like. I want to know why."

"Have a seat." He let the luggage straps slide off his shoulders.

"I don't want to sit."

"You will for this."

His tone stopped her and she slowly moved toward him. "Why did you want to see the hall outside Brogue's room?" She blinked when he suddenly bolted toward her.

Smoak took her by the arm and led her to the sofa. He sat before her on the coffee table.

"Brogue's dead." He brought his hands down on her thighs when she tried to bolt. "You can't go to him."

"How?" The word was hushed. Her eyes glistened with tears.

"He was murdered, Sweet." Smoak read her expression with ease. "I didn't do it," he said.

"Rain Su," Sabra recalled the woman from the camera footage. "I met her when she was hired. She looked like she could handle herself, but I don't think she could take down the likes of Brogue."

"She may know who did." Smoak fingered the hem of her dress. "She left his room around the time we think he was killed."

"We?"

"My father and uncle found him- they're taking care of it."

"Oh they are?" Sabra pushed his hands off her thighs. "You do realize none of you are in charge of a damn thing here?"

"We're not taking over." He squeezed the bend of her knee until she fidgeted. "You don't need any parts of this- you know that."

"What'd they do with him?"

"They'll arrange for him to be found but nowhere near here."

Her mouth trembled. She wanted to cry but she was hesitant to mourn Brogue's death in the presence of his cousin.

"Hey…" he pulled her close. "It's okay, it's okay…" he nodded when she set her emotions loose. "That's it," he soothed as her tears wet his shirt.

"I know you hated him…" her voice was a shudder. "But it wasn't all his fault, his father turned him into…"

A Lover's Hate

"I know," Smoak cupped her face and planted a hard kiss to her forehead.

She sniffled hard, disgusted then by her loss of control. "I need to go," she bristled against him.

"Sabra I need you to keep me in the loop about where you are at all times," he stayed seated on the coffee table and watched her leave the sofa. "I can't take a chance on you getting more involved in this than you already are."

She stopped just short of the living room entryway.

"I need to unpack," he left the table and went to her. "Why don't you get some rest?"

Sabra kept a hand over her mouth, fearing she'd break into another fit. She nodded. "I want to be alone Smoak."

He understood and pulled her back next to him to drop a kiss to her cheek. He followed her departure with a pensive glare.

***

It was past ten when Roman returned to the villa he and Imani shared. He found her in the lounge. She stood before the windows taking in the dazzling view of the city. Roman took his time then to just watch his wife- to treasure the sight of her *standing*. He bowed his head, flexing muscles along either side of his strong jaw as he gave thanks for her recovery.

Imani chose that moment to turn. Uncertainty guarded her exceptional features.

"Did Pitch tell you about Brogue?" He asked.

She blinked at the sound of his voice and then nodded. Despite their passionate reunion, the Tesanos had barely spoken to one another since.

"I know that in your world women aren't supposed to let on that they have working brains, but losing you over some vendetta isn't an option for me. I'm sorry that I was selfish. I made you suffer so I wouldn't have to." Imani let her eyes drift downward and then she moved toward one of the doorways leading out of the room.

"I'm sorry too Immi," Roman called and waited for her to look his way again. "I promised myself and your family that I'd never give you cause to be afraid of me and I did that."

A frown creased Imani's brow. "I'm not afraid of you Roman."

"You're afraid of what I'll do." He walked over to her. "In my book, that's the same thing." He ran the back of his hand down her arm and tugged the hem of the sleep shirt she'd lounged in that day.

"Roman…"

"I don't want to argue anymore Immi."

His fingers were grazing her inner thigh and Imani was ready to give in. She resisted.

"If you mean that, then I should tell you the rest of it."

Her words darkened his bottomless stare. "What rest?" He asked.

"I didn't do this just to keep you safe." Her eyes shimmered defiantly then. "I'd want someone to do the same for our sons."

"What are you talking about Immi?"

"He was a child, Ro. Groomed to be a monster, *by* a monster. He could've been a better man. I saw it in his eyes that day."

Roman gripped Imani's hands and tugged. "What are you saying to me?"

"Your brother sent his son to do his dirty work. Brogue put me in that chair."

A Lover's Hate

***

Smoak had done a hasty job of settling in but he decided it was good enough. He was more interested in getting back to Sabra. Not that she'd welcome him into her bedroom. He heard her set the lock when she went inside earlier. She wouldn't grant admission easily- or at all, to him.

Choosing not to dwell on that, Smoak focused his energies on other matters. He found his phone and located the number he needed. While waiting for the connection, he studied the security footage photos.

"Dean Warkowski," a voice answered.

"D!"

"Smoak, man! How was the wedding?"

"A good time was had by all."

"Ha! That's sayin' a lot when family is involved." The Phoenix police detective mused.

"Damn right it is," Smoak laughed. "Listen D, I'm sorry for bothering you so late."

"Don't worry about it. I'm still here at the station."

"Anything new on the hit and run comin' to see me?"

"It's all been pretty much a dead end-pun intended." Dean groaned. "We still went through the motions, lookin' for any family he may've had. Burial purposes, you know?"

"Anything turn up?"

"If you count records for school attendance and foster care, but then it's like the guy just dropped off the face of the earth- resurfaced about six or seven years ago following some exhibition. Seems he was some kind of artist."

AlTonya Washington

Smoak scanned the security pictures again. "You find any clues at the accident site?"

"More weirdness," Dean said, "had it not been for the tire marks on the guy's chest, it would've looked like an accident. Whoever did this didn't want us to misunderstand. They wanted us to know the guy was murdered." He chuckled shortly, but there was more agitation than amusement in the sound.

"It's a good thing they left such a blatant clue since we missed the other one."

Smoak looked away from the photos. "What other one?"

"M.E. found a pin prick in the guy's chest- drove us crazy for weeks. Finally we realized they stuck the thing right in the poor bastard's chest- a note."

Smoak had already guessed the contents of the note before Dean recited.

"'For your attention, E'."

***

Rain Su poured a third glass of the full-bodied cabernet and settled back into the cushions along the base of the sofa. She enjoyed the next movement of the Schubert arrangement until the phone vibrated with the text she'd been waiting on. She dialed the number given in the message.

"It's done," she said once the call connected.

There was hesitation followed by a woman's soft breathy laughter. "Thank you Rain. I wish I could've been there to see it."

"Trust me," Rain purred, "the asshole knew why his throat was being cut. I chanted your name while my blade spilled his blood."

"Was the note someplace sure to be found?"

"Yes," Rain laughed, "oh yes…"

"Well then, that'll have to do. Guess it's on to the next one."

Rain lifted her wine glass in toast. "So how do you want me to handle it?"

"I don't."

Rain straightened so quickly she almost spilled the remainder of her wine. "You're not going to let Maeva-"

"Jesus no. Never again. My sister's…talents are best used elsewhere."

"Yeah," Rain relaxed a little, "that's what we thought when you sent her to keep an eye on Sabra Ramsey."

"Well it all turned out in the end."

Rain appeared distressed then. "I think they have my face. That resort had unbelievable security."

"I was actually counting on that, hon. It wouldn't do for us to be completely anonymous."

"So who's on the next one?" Rain asked.

More breathy laughter followed the question before the woman replied. "The next one is all mine."

NINETEEN

Smoak left Sabra with her privacy for the duration of the evening. He needed the time alone probably as badly as she did. Unfortunately, time spent mulling over all the new developments uncovered during the last week and a half had done little to offer more clarifications. If anything, he had even more questions.

Since he had the run of the large stunning apartment Smoak turned in pretty late. He didn't worry that Sabra kept to her room. From time to time he could hear her moving around. The sound of music radiated just barely past the walls of her bedroom. His visit there two nights before told him the place was stocked with everything she'd need to hold up there for at least a week. Still, he'd have given anything to see her trussed up in the fur-lined cuffs hanging from the chains attached to that monstrously huge bed of hers.

A Lover's Hate

He woke that morning and decided to prepare breakfast for them both. While it was customary for him to go without clothing when he was home, he reminded himself that he wasn't home- yet. He donned a pair of black fitted boxers before leaving the guest room. It was a good move on his part, for he and Sabra weren't alone in the apartment.

Smoak was heading into the kitchen when he heard a door open. Sounds from the TV spilled out of a room on the other side. Curious, Smoak waited. He was somewhat shielded from view but made no real attempt to mask his presence. He heard movement and expected to see Sabra. He wasn't all that surprised to see Lee Lee Arnold leaving the room and in sleep attire. He considered that for a few seconds and then continued his path into the kitchen.

Sabra left her room shortly after Lee Lee's departure. Aromas of breakfast had seeped under the doorway and proved to be irresistible. She found Smoak at the stove; his back was turned to her as she entered. Heart slamming against her ribs, she studied the ripple and flex of sinewy muscle beneath the flawless black of his skin.

Pressing her lips together, Sabra did her best to maintain silence. She padded slowly toward him to determine whether his back was all that was bared. The sigh she uttered held faint traces of disappointment when she noticed the underwear hugging his lean waist and perfect ass.

"Morning," Smoak greeted when he heard her sigh. "Hungry?" He asked without turning away from the stove.

"I didn't know I had enough to make a decent meal," she said looking at the bowls and pans he used.

"More than enough," he laughed.

"Oh well," she moved on into the kitchen, "guess we have Lee to thank for that."

Smoak took advantage of the opening. "You guys are still close," he noted.

"I trust her with my life."

"Close since college, huh?"

"Mmm hmm," Sabra went to help herself to freshly brewed coffee.

"I'm surprised she didn't spit in my face when I came to town," he idly noted while turning the heat down under the omelets he'd prepared.

Sabra paused while adding cream to her coffee. "Why the hell would she do that?"

Smoak didn't answer, keeping his focus on washing out a mixing bowl.

Sabra observed the set of his profile and read his expression. "She understood."

"How could she?"

Sabra finished adding the cream to the coffee mug. "It's a long story."

"Clearly we've got time," he waved toward his boxers and the tank top and yoga pants she wore.

Instead, Sabra took her coffee and made a mad dash around the chrome cooking island. "Call me when breakfast's ready." She said over her shoulder.

Smoak curved his hands over the black chrome rim of the sink. His fist hit the countertop when her room door slammed.

***

Smoak took breakfast in the guest room while Sabra dined in her bedroom. They avoided each other for the rest of the morning. Smoak had a shower, dressed and left the

A Lover's Hate

apartment an hour before Sabra. He charted a direct path to Lee Lee Arnold's office.

It was still pretty early in the morning. The corridors along the executive wing were relatively quiet. Smoak could hear the sounds of a network morning show coming through the open door of Lee's office. He found the woman perched on the corner of a pristine white oak desk. Her square-toed pumps were discarded on the floor near the sofa in the living area along with a short-waist blazer from the pin-striped lilac pantsuit.

He dropped a single knock to the open door and gave a half smirk when Lee Lee jumped at the sight of him filling her doorway.

"Smoak," she reached for the remote and lowered the volume on the TV. "The architects are okay with rescheduling the meeting we moved yesterday."

"Whatever you set up is fine," he studied the circular moves of his thumb against his palm then. "That's not why I'm here," he said.

"Oh?" Lee Lee surmised that the approaching conversation would require her to be fully suited and at the ready. She eased off the desk to slip on her shoes and blazer.

"Saw you on your way out this morning." Smoak moved into the office. "Didn't realize you and Sabe got started so early. Or maybe you were finishing up late?"

Tilting her head, Lee watched Smoak curiously. "She um…told me you'd taken the guest room."

"Is that a problem for you?"

"Me?" Surprise merged with Lee Lee's curiosity. "No…why?"

Smoak casually tugged the rolled cuffs of his shirt and went to lean on the desk. "The way I just dropped in on

your girl, made my presence known," he shrugged.
"Despite all the time that's passed between us, I came here
with an agenda and a shitload of possessiveness in place
anyway."

Lee fixed him with an easy smile. "I haven't heard
Sabra complaining much."

"And what about you?"

"Um...Smoak I'm sorry I..." Lee clasped her hands
and extended them in his direction. "I'm confused. What
are you trying to say?"

"I've seen the chains on her bed Lee Lee."

Confusion remained for only another few seconds.
Then, a combination of unease and amusement filled Lee's
light eyes. She covered her mouth and slowly walked to the
other side of the bright room.

Smoak expelled the breath he didn't realize he was
holding. A fair amount of unease sharpened his striking
profile when he stood from the desk and went to observe
the view from the windows. "Sorry for embarrassing you
Lee, but this is new to me too. I um..." he grimaced at the
uncharacteristic stumbling over words. "I apologize for
overstepping here Lee but I uh...I've got a right to know if
I'm not the only one..." he cleared his throat then, inwardly
celebrating the end of the uncomfortable speech.

Lee had turned to watch him as he struggled to
share the explanation. No wonder her best friend had never
been able to get the man out of her system. He had an
uncanny talent for coming across as dangerous and
unapproachable yet vulnerable and humble in the same
vein.

"Smoak?" She waited for him to turn and see the
humor in her expression. "I'm flattered that you think
I'm...capable of competing with *you* for Sabra's affection,"

A Lover's Hate

she let him see the feminine adoration in her eyes. "But I swear you've got it wrong. This isn't about what you think. There's nothing sexual going on between us."

Lee Lee's gaze was direct- its meaning clear and genuine. Smoak appeared to relax just slightly. He nodded slowly as though what she said had convinced him. Her words however did nothing to settle the questions surging through his mind. Lee Lee must have sensed that, for she raised both hands to stop him before he could speak.

"If you want to know anything else, you'll have to ask Sabra."

Smoak bowed his head and spared time for a short laugh. "I think you know she won't tell me a damn thing."

"I think you're wrong about that," Lee sighed and moved toward her desk. "Maybe you should try observing her first."

"Observing," Smoak read Lee Lee's resolute nod and knew she'd offer no more insights.

"It'd be best to do that where you won't be disturbed. Her place on the lake is best," Lee brushed her fingers across her brow as she shared the information. "It's cleaned once a week, fully stocked with food...you could stay until you get the answers you want."

"How will I know if she's being straight with me?"

"You'll know. And you won't doubt it." She returned to perch on the corner of the desk. "Keys are in the bottom drawer next to the fridge in the penthouse kitchen. It'd be best if you don't tell her you're headed out there. She's not too keen on spending time there unless the place is full of people."

Smoak felt the urge to smile for the first time that morning. "So why'd she buy it?"

AlTonya Washington

Lee only spread her hands. "This is Sabra we're talkin' about."

He chuckled then, nodding his understanding. "Thanks Lee," he said and took his leave.

TWENTY

Lake Tahoe, Nevada~

"What are we doing here Smoak?" Sabra's voice held the same flat tone that it'd carried since the chopper had set down on the airstrip.

When he led her up to the tower roof that morning he'd said the sudden trip had to do with the upcoming construction on the resort property. He didn't seem to be in the mood for taking no for an answer.

He'd even lightly threatened her with using more land than he'd initially requested for the project. Given the fact that he was then only using a fraction of the property that was lawfully his, Sabra decided it would be foolish to argue further. As for not questioning their purpose for being in Lake Tahoe, she was damn well going to have her answers.

A Lover's Hate

She'd already questioned him four times since they'd left the airstrip in the Chevy Half Ton he'd secured. When they took the private winding road leading to her home, she inquired yet again and heard the faintest tremor in her voice as the mansion came into view.

The beauty of the gray brick dwelling never failed to stop her breath despite the fact that she rarely spent time there. She'd acquired it to build her asset portfolio and to impress the hell out of whoever was lucky enough to be granted an invitation to one of the few events she held there during the year.

"Smoak-" Her voice echoed in the spacious cab when he shut down the truck's engine. He'd parked along the outer edge of the curved driveway.

He gave her the full benefit of his attention then. "Would you please relax?"

"You shouldn't have brought me here if you want me to relax."

Smoak propped his elbow on the steering wheel and grinned. "Tell me you're not shallow enough to buy a house like this and not use it?"

Sabra clasped her hands in her lap. "Okay."

His laughter resounded rich and contagious- Contagious to anyone besides Sabra. She looked ready to jump from her skin.

Sobering some, Smoak fingered a lock of her hair. "Why don't you like the house?"

"It's a beautiful house," she sighed smoothing both hands across her thighs bare past the hem of the casual deep purple jersey dress. "Wait 'til you get around back and see the lake…the mountains in the distance."

"Sounds exquisite, which doesn't explain why you're so," he trailed a finger down her cheek and watched her flinch, "jumpy," he observed.

"I just don't like to be here alone."

"Honey you're not alone," he reminded her in the gentlest of tones. For the first time that morning, he witnessed her features softening with relief. He graced her with a sly wink and then left the truck.

"Give me a tour?" He offered his arm and watched her take it as she would a lifeline.

Sabra's flair for space and subtle lighting came through across every part of the 20,000 square foot dwelling. Smoak was impressed when she told him that attention to light and space were the only demands she made of the architects before she had the place built. Smoak mentioned that such sprawling property couldn't have been easy to come by out there, Sabra surprised him by revealing the fact that his uncles were the original owners.

"Uncle West acquired it in a land deal with them," she said as they made way for the wide stone steps leading to the front door. "After we got the property in Vegas, I came to appreciate its worth," she shrugged in spite of herself.

"I talked to my Uncle West about putting more money into real estate and voila."

"Smart lady," Smoak observed as he surveyed the sheer scale of the house.

"I'm sure *that's* a surprise."

Smiling at her sarcasm, Smoak unlocked the front door but held her against the jamb before she could clear the threshold. "Not at all," he argued and dipped his head.

A Lover's Hate

Their kiss grew heated in the span of a second. As it was customary, something fierce ignited between them.

"Dammit," he snapped, "why are your clothes so easy to get into?"

She cried out when he'd reached beneath her dress and clutched her ass. His thumb began a savage assault on her clit outlined against the lacy crotch of her panties. "More complaints about my clothes, hmm?" She groaned as he swept her off her feet and kicked the door shut.

"Not at all," he murmured against her earlobe before drawing the flesh between his teeth.

He had her half out of the seductively cut dress by the time he'd found his way to a massive staircase shielded behind a portrait lined wall. He whispered for directions to the bedroom while ascending the curving oak case that branched off at the top.

Only a strapless black bra and matching panties adorned Sabra's body when Smoak cleared the doorway to the master bedroom suite. There, he dropped her onto the bed and followed her down. He relieved her of her underwear and the spike-heeled purple sandals that accentuated her pedicure and devastating length of her legs.

His mouth followed the path of his hands. He worshipped the fullness of her cleavage. Still, he spent the greatest portion of his time savoring the softness of her inner thighs and the treasure that lay between.

"Take off your clothes," she curved her nails into the stark white T-shirt partly visible beneath the blue-checked gingham shirt he sported.

"This'll be over too soon if I do that," he admitted, moments before nuzzling his nose past the petals guarding her sex. He infrequently dipped his tongue to taste the moisture rich cavern of sensation.

AlTonya Washington

Sabra raked her nails over his head, grinding into the subtle thrusts he made inside her body.

"Please?" She gave an insistent tug to the shirt tails hanging outside his dark blue denims. "Smoak-"

Sabra's pleas ended on a moan and her focus then was on drinking her taste from his mouth when he kissed her. While she was absorbed in that act, Smoak came out of his top shirt. Muscles flexed wickedly as he worked it off his back. The T-shirt was next to go. Sabra moved against his fist when she felt it press into her as he released the fly of his jeans. He tugged the garment just over his butt until he'd freed the erection from his boxers.

She laughed breathlessly when he took her thighs and pulled her down to the center of the bed. She bit her lip on the blissful sensation of his thick shaft invading the part of her anatomy that most yearned for it.

Smoak lifted his head to watch her face as he claimed her with slow, relentlessly penetrating strokes. His heart thudded in his ears and his eyelids grew heavy from the pleasure of her coating his dick with her need. He settled his face into the crook of her neck and gave into what was all but setting him aflame. He clutched her thighs, setting them further apart. His thrusts turned hungrier, more demanding as she gloved and released his sex until she'd finished him.

They lay in silence for a time. Only the sounds of their mutual breathing filled the room until the hum of the central cooling system added itself to the mix. After a while, Smoak began to withdraw and Sabra locked her legs around his back to forbid it.

"I should get our stuff from the truck before it gets any later." He murmured into her neck.

Sabra relaxed her legs a little. "Is this *you* concerned about clothes?"

"Maybe I'm tryin' to turn over a new leaf."

Sabra pressed against his chest. "What for?" her appraisal was obvious as her eyes followed the movement of her fingers trailing his awesome chest.

"Thank you," he smiled at her unspoken compliment and leaned in to nibble her earlobe until he felt the stream of additional moisture on his semi-hard arousal.

"Get some rest Sweet." He advised, squeezing her chin when he looked down at her. "You'll need it."

She argued even as drowsiness claimed her. Mumbles of disapproval faded into silence when she drifted off. Smoak tucked her in and left her to sleep.

***

Smoak retrieved their belongings from the truck but decided not to return to the master bedroom. He took one of the guest rooms on the same wing and got a little work done while Sabra slept. He had put in a few productive hours before hunger called and he figured a late supper would do them both some good.

He was setting out for the kitchen when Sabra emerged naked from her room. Smoak guessed she'd had the same idea for eating and celebrated her intention to do it in the buff. He followed her down the long corridor-golden lit by electric candles and leading toward the stairway. She seemed unaware of his presence behind her and Smoak enjoyed the sight of her nudity even as he toyed with a devilish idea to give her a playful scare when she got to the stairs.

Instead of *him* scaring *her* though, Sabra was the one who sent his heart plummeting. She'd stumbled on the first step on the opulent staircase. Smoak broke into a sprint

AlTonya Washington

and then looked on in horrified disbelief when she grasped the square newel post and steadied herself.

He slowed his run and was opening his mouth to call out to her, but something stopped him. Silently, he watched her make her way down the rest of the curving case. He didn't touch her, but remained close in case she lost her footing again.

On the main floor, she headed for the den and then changed her mind. Instead, she moved toward the living room. Again, she changed her mind and went to the kitchen.

Smoak's brows drew into a curious frown as he followed her. She bumped into a chair set under the small mahogany dining table just inside the kitchen. She didn't take time to straighten the chair or even to look back at it when she passed.

She moved deeper into the kitchen, only bumping lightly against the cooking island before she reached the towering refrigerator. She opened it and Smoak waited for her to retrieve a bottle of something alcoholic. He had a feeling though that alcohol wasn't her reason for being there.

Sabra stared into the refrigerator for well over two minutes. Smoak flipped the overhead kitchen lights once on and then off. Sabra didn't turn. Whatever held her fascination inside the refrigerator, it was powerfully strong.

Smoak began to close the distance separating them. For good measure, he reached up to tap at the stainless steel pots hanging from the iron rack above the island.

Sabra didn't turn to acknowledge him or the racket made by the pots. Smoak bowed his head for a second or two as though he were debating, second-guessing his next move. Grinding his jaw resolvedly, he reached out to draw hair away from the crook of her neck. He kissed her there.

Sabra tilted her head up as if her attention had finally been pulled from the fridge. She turned and; without a word, kissed him hard and full across the mouth.

Smoak didn't resist…at first. He wanted to ask her what was wrong, but didn't have the chance. Her kiss grew hungrier with every stroke of her tongue and he was; of course, affected. He moved to shut the door at her back; his intention was to carry her upstairs.

He wasn't given the opportunity to do that either. Sabra was pushing him away from the refrigerator. She didn't stop until the island prevented further movement once she had Smoak against it. The suspicions that had niggled at him for over a year began to take root.

"Sabra? Baby come upstairs with me." He softly encouraged amidst their kiss. His hands closed over her arms but she wrenched free and shoved his chest. He put his hands to her waist and squeezed. When she slapped his forearm, he overpowered her, setting her back to look into her blank stare which gradually filtered with wickedness.

"Sabra."

She responded to the sound of her name with a slap to his jaw.

"Sabra."

She shoved him that time, until he moved from the island. When the wooden and metal structure was no longer a barrier, she pressed down on his shoulders. Tugging at his wrists, she went to her knees and carried him with her to the floor in front of the refrigerator. She pushed until he was on his back.

Smoak continued to call out to her softly. Somehow he knew anything more forceful would not be a good idea.

AlTonya Washington

His whispers however grew faint as he was captivated by the sometimes blank, sometimes wicked gleam that crept in and out of her rich toffee eyes.

He couldn't judge her reaction to the fact that he was already naked. Her nails were raking his skin and she seemed to be of a mind to rip off whatever it was he wore.

"Sabra," he squeezed her bare thighs.

He made a slight move to topple her and she slapped him full across the face. Then, she fell over him gnawing the line of his collarbone before soothing the area with her tongue.

He was cupping her ass then, but not to unsettle her. Sabra had already taken him inside her and he had no will to deny anything she wanted. She wound herself above his hips while burying her fingers in her hair. Then she bit her lip and rode him hard, intent on fulfilling her own needs.

Smoak didn't mind. He let her expel what drove her, pleased to provide the platform for her venting. His very long lashes drifted to shield his stare but he couldn't look away from her- beautiful, wild and in total control of the act taking place between them there on the floor.

The refrigerator churned out cool air but their dark bodies were sweat-drenched, glistening from the appliance light as they were engulfed in erotic elation.

TWENTY-ONE

Morning arrived, different to tell from the master bedroom suite which was still closed to the outside world. Only the shallow light from the wardrobe room across the suite provided a hint of illumination. The crystal encased clock on the nightstand read 12:20pm when Sabra showed the first signs of stirring from her deep slumber.

It took some time before her eyes opened fully. When they did, they sparkled with something that was unmistakably haunted. She blinked and blinked again when she recognized the muscled wall of flesh at her back.

Contentment surged when Smoak pushed her hair aside and let his mouth graze her nape.

"Smoak," her voice was slow, lazy and she could have cuddled back into the welcoming embrace of sleep were it not for that which haunted her.

A Lover's Hate

If Smoak was there in her bed, chances were he'd been there the entire night. She'd never slept in that bed the entire night...not really.

He propped his chin on her shoulder. "You sleepwalk, don't you?"

Somehow, contentment returned as his words registered in her psyche. She nodded.

"Was it...was it because of what I did? That day-"

"No, *no*." She breathed and turned on her other side to face him. "I've tried to tell you it wasn't your fault-"

"But you didn't tell me this Sabra. You didn't tell me *this*." He cupped her chin to keep her eyes on his.

Her stare wavered anyway before it faltered all together.

"How long?" Smoak asked after silence rested between them for a short while.

"Longer than I want to remember."

Her hollow admission made him sit up and pull her with him. He tilted his head then, determined to maintain his observance of her face. He pushed at the lengthy tendrils that draped her shoulders and curtained her expression.

"Please talk to me, babe. I love you," his mouth glided her brow where he placed a kiss. "This is about to drive me out of my mind," he said. "I'm terrified for you," he felt the slightest movement of her shoulders before she gave in to a powerful bout of trembling. When she cried, he kissed away her tears as quickly as they fell.

"Talk to me," he hugged her tight giving her an encouraging shake in the process. "Did Brogue do something?"

Sabra shook her head, cradled in his neck while she sobbed. "It wasn't your cousin. It was his father."

"Gabriel." Smoak's face changed then. His features lost none of their magnificence moreover they were enhanced by reignited scorn. He let go of Sabra then, fearing he'd crush her out of rage. "Tell me," he said.

"I thought I'd beaten it," Sabra focused on her hands clenching fists to stop their shaking. "I went through all of high school without an episode."

"How long did it go on before that?"

She moved her hands across the rumpled covers. "Since I was ten."

"And when did it start again?"

"When Quest introduced me to Pike...*Tesano*." She squeezed her eyes shut. "When I heard the name, everything changed. I met you next," she smiled, the gesture was a mix of delight and sadness. "Then Brogue and then his dad." She pulled at the top sheet and balled her fists inside the linen.

"Drinking helped, but not for long. I thank God for making Lee Lee my roommate." She breathed.

"What did Gabriel do?"

Smoak's voice held an odd softness and Sabra risked a quick glance up to see that his features were still drawn harsh.

"Nothing," she replied flatly. "He didn't *do* anything to me he...he threatened me when I was a child."

Smoak shut his eyes. "Son of a fucking bitch," he drew a fist across his hair.

Sabra kept her head down. "Are you sure you want to hear this?"

The bed shifted beneath Smoak's weight and he moved close to her again.

"Yes." He kissed her shoulder.

A Lover's Hate

Sabra propped against the towering headboard and drew her knees up to her chest.

"My parents argued all the time. They never agreed on one thing-not one especially my mother's job. Uncle West gave her the PR department at Ramsey- the place is what it is today because of her. Hmph, folks at Ramsey still call to get her opinions."

Smoak grinned. "Bet she loves that."

"She certainly doesn't hate it." Sabra mused. "She got me the best nannies money could buy so she could devote all her time to that place." The memories dimmed her expression again. "There was one- Aiesha Yale. She was my favorite. She was young- well closer to my age than any of the others Mommy used. She was taking a couple of years off before college to save up so she didn't mind if Mommy worked her like a slave.

Besides," Sabra began to twirl a lock of her hair and studied the tendril as it looped her finger, "she got the chance to act like the queen of a castle when Mommy wasn't home which was a lot. Aiesha would dress up in Mommy's stuff but she was so neat about it. She always put everything back more perfect than Mommy and that was easy. Mommy never really worried about picking up after herself." She flashed Smoak a sly look then.

"If I had any ideas about telling on Aiesha, she could easily tell on me too since she never said anything about me playing in Mommy's makeup."

Smoak's laughter was soft and easy as he watched the woman he loved recall the more lighthearted aspects of her childhood. "Aiesha sounds smart," he noted.

"She was," Sabra clasped her hands atop her knees and studied her thumbs one rolling over the other. "Maybe she was *too* smart. She was decked out in my mother's best slut-wear the night your uncle came to the house to see Mommy about business." The memory made Sabra twist her nose in distaste.

"I'm sure it was something that could've waited, but he had a thing for my mom." She dismissed the thought with a wicked eye roll. "Mommy and Daddy were out on the town- it was one of their getting along periods." She shrugged. "Daddy never liked your uncle."

Smoak nodded approvingly. "Good for Mr. Felix."

Sabra didn't give into the humor his cheer stoked. "I guess Aiesha was good enough for what he had in mind that night. They'd met before so I'm not sure that was their 'first time'." She curved the index and middle fingers on both hands to quote the phrase.

"It's alright," Smoak encouraged when she put her forehead to her knees and shuddered.

"I woke up...hearing them," she sent him a pointed look when she raised her head. "I got up and saw Aiesha in her room with him. Her arms were tied to one of the canopy posts on her bed. She and your uncle...but he wasn't hurting her. She was laughing and then she saw me watching. She started to struggle and he must've thought it was part of whatever game they were playing. I saw him slapping her face, but she was laughing over it... until she saw me.

He got more aggressive the more she struggled," Again, Sabra put her head to her knees, squeezing her eyes then as if to ward off the images that refused to remain at bay. She tugged the sheets over her shoulders.

"When he was finished, he finally paid attention to the look on her face and then he saw me too. I may've been eleven, come to think of it..." she shook off the inconsequential detail. "He walked over and stooped down in front of me- he told me I should never tell what I saw or he-he'd do the same to my mother, my father, me…Aiesha was already or about to be eighteen so I guess he couldn't go to jail."

She nodded with decisive slowness. "I believed him. I believed he'd come back to do what he promised. Mommy believed it too."

Smoak tucked her into his warmth when her tears took hold again. He kissed her temple and whispered soothing words into her hair.

"I know I wasn't supposed to say anything," Sabra's voice muffled into Smoak's shoulder and then she hid her face in his neck. "I wet my bed that night. I was eleven! Mommy was pissed and scared and I-just blurted it out. Aiesha was already cleaned up by the time her and Daddy got back. They didn't suspect a thing."

"Mommy never had the chance to confront Aiesha. She left right after they got home. I never saw her again." She pressed at Smoak's chest then, swiping wetness from her cheeks with the backs of her hands.

"My sleep patterns were for shit after that. Mommy wouldn't risk getting help for my sleepwalking or anything else. If Daddy found out, he would've taken me for sure. If anyone else found out…" her mouth thinned. "Your uncle could've come back."

Smoak was sitting in the corner of the bed, one leg folded, the other raised where he propped his elbow and massaged his fingers across the pain dancing across his temple. He could actually feel weakness unexpectedly surging to parallel the fury that threatened to consume him. He wouldn't give into it.

"Tell me about the chains," he asked, rubbing his eyes. When there was silence, he looked her way and smiled. "I've seen them, Sweet."

Sabra pressed the heels of her hands into her eyes and groaned. "Lee Lee's idea." She let her hands fall and studied the bedroom's vaulted ceiling. "Drinking to sleep isn't a good idea- at least it wasn't for me. We didn't know what to do after we tried that. I'd get up wearing nothing and just leave the room. Farthest I ever got was the dorm lobby. Thank God Lee Lee was a light sleeper. It only got me in trouble a few times.

First was with one of Fernando's friends who lived in our dorm." She glanced Smoak's way, clearing her throat when she spied the venomous set to his striking profile. "It was just my luck having my cousin stop by that night. Fernando went crazy when he found me there- almost killed the guy who didn't come back to school after the beating he took. Then, there was the pass at Lee Lee," she covered her face out of embarrassment. "She came up with the idea for the bed ties the next day."

The admission brought amusement to Smoak's expression. Laughter merged and he and Sabra indulged for a time.

"Was there another time?" He tangled his fingers with hers.

She nodded. "I didn't even realize there *had* been another time until I talked to Brogue a few days ago." She squeezed Smoak's hand as if to retrieve strength. "I went over to his apartment just to talk. His dad was there and we met...officially. He hadn't forgotten me. I could see it when he looked at me and I freaked. Brogue noticed. He came to my room later to check on me. Lee Lee went home that weekend and…If it hadn't been him…it would've been somebody else."

She looked at Smoak then, her eyes blurred by tears and pain. "I didn't set out to hurt you with him." Tears slid free again when he jerked her into a fierce embrace. "Using alcohol as the excuse always worked. Fernando believed it when he came down on me about his friend. Course it didn't stop him from beating the guy half to death."

"Do Belle and Bill know?"

"No. Mommy told Aunt Bri and Aunt Carm only about the sleepwalking but not why it started and she made them promise not to say anything to the kids. She didn't want anyone givin' me a hard time." She moved back from Smoak and folded her legs beneath her.

"Ty suspected…I think…she practically grew up with us. She was easy to talk to about my parent's drama. But I never told her the rest of it."

Smoak scanned the bedroom then. "Why don't you stay here alone?"

Sabra drew an invisible pattern into the covers. "That gorgeous lake out back- I walked right into it, almost drowned."

"Jesus Sabra," his whisper sounded vicious.

Sabra watched stoically as he moved shaking hands across his face. "I was planning for a party. I got here before Lee. She found one of the back doors open and came looking for me." Smiling then, she shrugged flippantly.

"Guess I can recall the elements of sex, but not swimming."

"That's not funny. You should've-"

"What? Called you?" She shook her head, knowingly. "I wasn't exactly on your list of favorite people then, was I?"

"Sabra I- I'm sorry for this."

She shook her head, easing a lock behind her ear. "Guess you'll keep saying that no matter how many times I tell you it's not your fault."

"You guess right." He reached for her hand again. "You're on my mind every day."

Sabra couldn't look at him then. His words had stunned her *that* much.

"I spent years punishing myself for being weak over still wanting you after you and Brogue… then I stopped pretending."

"When exactly?" Sabra asked, frowning a little. "We've been at each other's throats for years."

"Mmm hmm…" Smoak left the bed stark naked and massaging his neck. "Coward's way out," he said across his shoulders.

"I was *happier*-" He rolled his eyes when the word left his tongue. "Happier I guess just having you come to me every year and then leave before shit got ugly."

"Shit *always* got ugly," she studied her hands clasped in her lap. "Were you okay with us being that way forever? Do you know what *I've* been going through all these years thinking you hate me?"

"I know," he looked at her, but couldn't hold her gaze for long. "I know because I went through those same years accepting that you hated me because of what I did to you."

"Christ," Sabra breathed then scrubbed her hands across her face. Furious, she grabbed a pillow and threw it at Smoak's chest. "Do the people who contract you to design weapons know you're a fucking idiot? How can you think I hate you when I throw myself at you every chance I get?!" She moved to her knees and stripped the top sheet

A Lover's Hate

off the bed. "And put some clothes on, dammit!" She threw the cover at him next.

Grabbing her robe, she pulled it on while leaving the bed.

Smoak sat on an armchair with the sheet dragged across his lap. He was quiet for a long time as if he'd been blindsided by a new and completely unexpected point of view. Then he leaned back on the chair and appeared to concede her point.

"Would you believe that I was so sure I had to be right about what you felt, so deluded by it that I didn't trust myself to believe what you were offering was real?"

Sabra had curled into the embroidered high back chair near the French doors across the room. "Yeah...I'd believe it." Hadn't she been just as distrustful of his actions over the last several days?

"I was very young when I saw your uncle with Aiesha. It was confusing- I didn't know if Aiesha was scared or enjoying herself. It screwed with my head big time," she shook her disarrayed tresses for emphasis. "It's *still* screwing with my head big time. Do you remember our first time together Smoak?" She chewed her thumbnail after asking the question.

He was leaning over in the armchair then, elbows braced to his knees. The memory made him smile. "You were a virgin."

"And when did you know that?"

The smile thinned. "When you screamed."

Sex between them had always been fierce and unrestrained. Sabra had struck him as anything but an innocent.

"That's right." She looked toward the French doors but saw nothing beyond the gauzy cream drapes. "I've always been dominant, strong-willed…a *tad* overconfident."

Smoak relaxed back in the chair again. "And let's not forget bull-headed and stubborn."

"Takes one to know one," She retaliated and returned his smile. "My mother raised me to be all that, but the older I got I started wondering if it was my upbringing or what I saw Gabriel doing to Aiesha that fueled the dominance. I never put much stock in it until my afternoon with you. I liked it, Smoak." She confessed firmly so he wouldn't doubt it. "I liked it and that scared the hell out of me."

She scooted to the edge of the chair. "What happened that day was everything our sex life already was-fierce, extreme…but then there was something else." She worried the lacy stitching along the hem of her robe. "I'd lived my life being strong and that day I realized I didn't have to be in charge and in control all the time. I liked the way it felt to give into that and then you said you'd never touch me again and I…" her breathing expelled in a shudder.

"I never wanted anyone else but you. I couldn't stand the thought of another man having me that way. I've never remembered the times I *walk*- the times when sex is involved but I know during them *I'm* the dominant one.

Fernando's roommate- when he tried to tell Fern what really happened, I know it was true. If I were the guy…they would've called what I did rape. When Brogue told me how I was that night with him-that he knew I wasn't myself, I knew I'd been *walking* and that afternoon with you there was something else that wanted out and it was something that had everything to do with what I saw happening to Aiesha.

A Lover's Hate

Smoak, I haven't been with another man since that day," she smiled at the sheer disbelief radiating from his incredible face. "*That's* why I've been throwing myself at you all these years. We only ever met in Phoenix at a restaurant or your office at the lab and...then that night last year you came to my hotel. *Why* did you do that?"

His index finger rested alongside his temple as he watched her bare her soul and he'd never loved her more.

"I wanted to make sure everything was okay with you," he said, "my family wanted to draw me into the foal. Quest demolishing Ramsey's weapons division hit a lot of people hard and in different ways. My family is a bunch of racist fucks, but a skilled weapons designer is worth his weight in gold." He smoothed his palm across his fist and followed the movement with his dark eyes.

"I found out they were contacting you. I'm pretty sure they wanted me to know that. Wanted it to rattle me into calling you, which would push me to call them and give them the chance to lay out some impressive offer to draw me in-it's how they operate but I still didn't think much of it then."

He cinched the bed-sheet at his waist and left the armchair. "Then there was the weird visit from that bitch followed by what happened to Austin Chappell." He leaned against the dresser. "It was the way you looked at me though. That morning on the day you left Phoenix, I knew something wasn't right with you."

"Did we...?" She tried to ask if they'd slept together.

He understood and shook his head no.

"I assumed we just..." Sabra looked toward the bed. "I did something earlier- last night, didn't I?" The

232

AlTonya Washington

confirmation in his eyes made her double over in the chair. "Why did you let me do that to you?" she moaned.

"I needed to prove it to myself." He steeled himself from going to her as she agonized over another loss of her faculties. "I already suspected but I had no proof. And then there were other selfish reasons."

"What reasons?" Sabra saw him as a blur in her teary gaze.

"Are you serious?" Smoak folded his arms over his chest and turned his mouth downward as he shrugged. "Guess I just wanted you to have your way with me."

Tears spurted from her eyes as she laughed.

"Baby you need someone," he advised once her laughter had eased off. "You need to talk to someone-" he cut his words when she shook her head wildly. Leaving the dresser, he kneeled before her chair and held her tight until she stilled.

"I won't let you argue with me- not about this." He said.

"My business-"

"Will be fine. You've given your life to it but I think you see you're not able to keep this buried as well as you once did." He cuffed her neck in his hand and brushed his thumb across a plump cheek. "Trying to ignore this may be part of the problem, you know?"

"Your uncle…"

"You don't worry about him." His features regained some of the harsh element that hardened them.

Sabra didn't want to know what his words meant.

"Listen," he shook off the hard look, "I think you know Gabe isn't the threat to you that he once was."

"Well can't I talk to you?" her voice was small.

"No."

"Why?"

"Because I don't think I'd be a good therapist, Sweet."

Sabra sighed at the sly look he gave her. "Why not?" She persisted.

His hands cruised along her thighs. "I'd want you on my couch too much," he said.

"Well isn't that where I'm supposed to be?"

"As long as I can be there with you."

She continued to smile, but eventually her face crinkled in preparation for a big cry.

"Don't, Sweet," he soothed, pulling her head into his neck. "Shh…you know I love you. If you think I'll let you go through any more of this alone, forget it. I take care of what belongs to me," he turned his face into her hair and breathed in. "You're mine as much as I'm yours."

His words sent a shudder through Sabra that had nothing to do with unrest, submission or giving up a part of herself. It was the contentment that came from being valued and cared for.

"I love you and I've always been yours," she confessed, easing back to brush her thumbnail across the delicious curve of his mouth.

He nuzzled her ear. "I won't ever forget that again."

Their kiss was one of implicit need and devotion. Sabra felt her hands weaken and she could do little more than half curl them against the pects flexing beneath Smoak's blackberry skin. He trailed his lips along her jaw, down her neck to outline her collarbone with the tip of his tongue.

One fluid move brought Smoak to his feet. He lifted Sabra against him as the sheet fell from his lean hips to cover his ankles before he stepped away to take her with him to the bed. As was customary, he tugged her down to the middle, smiling when she bit her lip expectantly.

His attention fixed on getting her out of the robe, only got as far as peeling it from her shoulder. Then, he was enticed by the bared breast that taunted him. Sabra arched, filling his mouth with her abundant cleavage and grinding her hips on his when he devoured what she offered.

"Stop moving," his order was a growl against her flesh.

"I can't," she breathed.

He squeezed her derriere while nibbling the firming peaks of her breasts. "This won't last long if you don't stop."

She didn't stop only added more urgency to her moves. "Do you have somewhere to be?" She clutched his butt and drew him closer.

He groaned over the nipple he suckled. "I'm there," he said.

Sabra insinuated a hand between them and worked his erection until he whimpered. She teased him with her kiss, barely stroking his tongue with hers.

"You're not there yet," she playfully observed. She put him inside her and took him deep. "There…" she sighed. "Still want me to stop?"

Smoak Tesano's dark eyes sparkled with an intense brilliance that only love could instill. "Not ever, Sabra. Don't ever stop."

TWENTY-TWO

Outside Mt. Kisko, New York~

Smoak gave up trying to persuade Sabra to tell him what they were doing there. After three days in Lake Tahoe, they both realized the responsibilities of their lives could no longer be ignored. Therefore, he was understandably curious when they hopped a flight to New York and took the drive upstate to his parent's home.

"Is this payback for not telling you we were going to the lake?" He asked when Sabra parked the rented Crossover model at an angle on the brick driveway.

"This can't be payback since I told you exactly where we were going." She threw him a wink while removing the key from the ignition.

"Where we were going but not why," Smoak countered when she'd strolled around to the passenger side to open his door.

"This is one of those situations where actions speak louder than words," Sabra leaned against the open door, folding her arms over the black empire-waist blouse she wore with jeans. She watched him leave the car.

"What actions?"

"Jeez, you brainy types are impatient," She eased away before he could trap her against the door once he was standing in front of her.

"Don't do that. I've got my key," he said, noticing that she was about to ring the bell.

Sabra pulled the chime that dangled next to the door. "*Patience*," she sang that time.

"Mmm hmm," he gestured and pulled her back against him to glide his mouth across her cheek.

"Smoak…" She bit her lip and nudged her bottom against him when his hands spanned her waist. "This is your parent's house," she bumped her elbow against the iron abs covered by the T-shirt he wore.

"And this is *me* being patient," he was suckling her earlobe when the front door lock twisted.

The door opened. Smoak felt his knees turn to water at the sight of his mother standing on her own two feet. His lips parted while his entrancing stare widened in disbelief and amazement at once. He attempted to speak, but had somehow lost the ability.

"Mama-" his voice was barely a breath, but it was all he could muster.

Imani reached out to smooth the back of her hand along his cheek. "It's real, baby." She assured him.

Smoak was still in an utter state of disbelief. He braced his hands to either side of the door, fearing that at any moment he would be the one to lose the use of *his* legs.

Imani nodded to Sabra. "Let's get him inside."

AlTonya Washington

Using combined efforts, the women ushered Smoak into the living room. Roman was there, his smile was a knowing one as he stood appreciating his son's amazement.

"Mama…when…?" Was all Smoak managed to put together that time. His expression still harbored a fair amount of disbelief as he sat on the sofa and watched his mother…standing.

"Two years," Imani watched her son take the blow, "your father left for his office one day and we both forgot that my chair was in a room down the hall. He'd uh…carried me to bed the night before." She walked over to Roman and took a seat on the arm of the chair he occupied.   "I was fine until I had to go to the bathroom," she smiled when Roman covered her knee with his hand. "I crawled all the way there and then broke down crying when I realized I couldn't get myself on the…" She let her lashes float down over her eyes as the humiliating memory stopped her.

"I pounded my fist to my thigh and…it hurt!" She laughed breathlessly and then covered Roman's hand with her own. "I forgot about using the bathroom and sat there for the next ten minutes hitting and pinching myself. I don't know how much longer it was before I actually tried to move and I *could move!*" Imani left Roman's side to take Smoak's hand when he reached out to her. She kissed him and laughed again.

"Why didn't you tell us?" Smoak blinked profusely and sniffled on the sobs filling his throat.

Imani had to speak around emotions filling her as well. "At first I thought it was a fluke. I feared I'd wake up the next morning needing my chair again. It was at least a month before I felt comfortable enough to be without it and then I-" She bowed her head and remained that way for a time. "I was afraid…that your father would do what he promised. No matter what he thought his brother had done, I didn't want Gabriel's blood on my hands."

"Why would you want to protect him, Miss Imani?" Sabra asked from her perch on the arm of a chair across the room.

Imani's smile was softer. "Because Gabriel didn't run that truck off the road. It was Brogue, love."

Sabra raised both hands to her mouth when she gasped.

"I knew you wouldn't be able to handle me telling you that part of the story before."

"Wait," Smoak's dark eyes narrowed when they slid from his mother to Sabra. "You knew?"

Sabra barely nodded, unable to look at him then and she turned her head.

"It was purely by chance, my love." Imani brushed Smoak's thigh, bringing his focus back to her. "She wanted so much to tell you but I made her swear to keep it a secret. I didn't realize that your father had already guessed at it." She gave a resolved shrug.

"I'm so sorry, baby." Imani squeezed Smoak's thigh as regret claimed her. "I never meant to keep this for so long- to lie to the people I love most." Her eyes filled with fresh tears. "And I do love you all so much, so very much-*too* much to risk losing you over some need for revenge-"

Smoak had pulled Imani into a fierce hug that cut off the rest of her speech. Mother and son remained locked in the embrace for a long time.

Across the room, Roman caught Sabra's eye and sent her a wink. "What do you say we give these two some time alone?" He asked.

AlTonya Washington

Sabra nodded, easing from the chair and waiting for Roman to join her at the front of the room. She happily accepted the arm he offered, eager to leave behind her worries.

***

Roman had taken Sabra on a walk around the lovely wooded grounds surrounding the house. Their trek ended at the lush flower garden where Imani had toiled; unbeknownst to her husband, while she tested the returning strength of her legs. Sabra could understand why the woman was drawn to the place with its fragrant beauty and serene appeal. She asked Roman to leave her there and was content to remain until she felt Smoak's hand in her hair. She indulged in only a few moments of the pleasure stemming from his touch and then decided it was time to face the music when his hand curved about her neck.

"Come to strangle me?" She asked, trying to work lightness into her voice.

Smoak let his mouth join his hand at Sabra's neck. He kissed her there. "Come to thank you."

She half turned on the stone bench; one of three in the quiet garden, "you're not mad?" She watched him incredulously when he sat next to her.

"What for?" He asked.

She frowned. "Are you serious?"

"Are *you*?"

"I kept this from you," she shook her head and appeared hopeless. "Given everything else I've done… how can you not hate me all over again?"

Smoak leaned in to nuzzle his nose to her temple. "I never hated you," a smile triggered the narrowing of his eyes that time. "I hated that I let what I felt for my family bring you harm."

A Lover's Hate

Sabra closed her eyes, relief claiming her as her worries started to vanish. "I called Miss Immi and told her I couldn't do it, that I couldn't keep this from you. Thank God Mr. Rome figured it out."

Smoak pulled a curl from its clinging perch at her jaw. "Whatever the reason, I'm glad she told me. It wouldn't have been fair for her to let you carry this on your shoulders."

"That's what she said when we talked on the phone." Sabra fingered a tear from the corner of her eye. "I'm still sorry I kept it from you for as long as I did." She smiled when his laughter reached her ears.

"I guess you'll keep apologizing no matter how much I tell you it's not your fault?"

Sabra recognized his question as one she herself had thrown at him on several occasions. "Guess we're two of a kind, huh?"

"Glad you feel that way," he nodded and squeezed her hand, pressing a kiss to the back of it. "Cause I couldn't marry a woman who didn't understand me."

Sabra felt her breath stop in her throat.

"Who didn't get me," he continued ignoring her surprise as he focused on sliding a stunning chocolate diamond onto her ring finger.

"Who has a scary talent for keeping me sane while she's driving me out of my mind."

"Smoak-"

"Be my wife? Be my wife always? I love you." He said.

"When did you...when did you decide-"

"Before I left Phoenix."

"But..." Sabra could only gaze upon the ring in stupefied silence for long moments then she gave a shake of her head. "Smoak are you sure? You really want me to be that-your wife? To be that in your life?"

"Do you love me, Sweet?"

She laughed, really laughed then. Joy; she'd never dreamed of for herself, was then promising to steal her breath.

"I love you," she gasped, "more than I can say, I love you."

"Then *show* me. Marry me." Smoak brushed at the happy tears that slipped from her eyes. "All I need is one word from you."

Sabra cupped his face and brought him closer. "I'll give you two words: yes and when?" She spoke against his mouth and then joined him in the laughter inspired by their love and its triumph over all that had kept them apart.

EPILOGUE

Paris, France~

The Ramseys and the DeBurghs had been enjoying the exquisite offerings found in the world's most romantic city. The two couples had partaken extensively of the Paris nightlife. Club hopping and restaurant visits had comprised the bulk of their trip.

Kraven and Darby had as much fun as the newlyweds. Given their busy schedules, the DeBurghs took advantage of having fun and rediscovering the reasons they fell in love. As for Fernando and Contessa, their already lavish and exciting honeymoon continued to provide a never ending array of delights. Naturally, the couple fully indulged.

Such unending excitement however, had its price. By the end of the week, both couples were feeling the effects of hard partying.

"Ah…damn…Whose idea was it to come out for breakfast?" Contessa was holding her head in her hands.

Darby was rolling her neck to work out the kinks. "I think it was my husband's idea," she muttered groggily.

"Hmph," County grimaced and rubbed her eyes. "I knew there was somethin' I liked about that guy."

"Hush," Darby tugged on the fuzzy cuffs of her cream sweater, "give my man a break, will you? He's been working non-stop for weeks. Whereas some of us"; she gave County a pointed look, "have been doing other things…non-stop."

County's smile was both lazy and wicked. "And that, was *my* husband's idea."

The women were still laughing when Kraven and Fernando arrived with steaming mugs of café mocha. The men announced that the orders were placed and would be arriving soon.

Darby shrugged toward County. "At least getting up at the ass crack of dawn gets us cute waiters."

The guys set the mugs to the small round tables the group had claimed outside the café. Though there was a definite nip in the air, the scrumptious café mochas and incomparable view made it all worth it.

Fernando remained standing while Kraven took his seat next to Darby.

"Wimpin' out on me, Count?" Fernando teased his wife.

"Still tough enough to outlast *you,* Ramsey."

"Mmm…that's not what you said last night."

Laughter rang out among the foursome. County left her seat and approached her husband. She jerked the hood on his navy fleece pullover and then they fell into a kiss.

Kraven and Darby were already in the midst of one. The kissing couples were interrupted by the sound of a throat clearing. The server had arrived with fresh baked croissants and an array of flavored butters and jams. When the stocky, stiff-backed gentleman stalked away, the group dissolved into more laughter.

"So are you two coming back to Scotland with Darby and me?" Kraven asked once they'd all somewhat sobered from their raucous behavior.

The Ramseys linked arms about each other's waists and looked down at Kraven. Fernando gave an exaggerated shrug.

"Depends on my wife. She's the one with the day job,"

County rolled her eyes, pretending to be inconvenienced. "Not even married two months and I'm already supporting the dead beat."

"Ah, come on Count," Fernando patted her waist. "You know I earn my keep."

The newlyweds fell into another kiss. Kraven and Darby shrugged, deciding it was no hardship to follow the example. Darby gasped suddenly, but it wasn't in response to the searing kiss she shared with her husband. She pulled back from Kraven, her eyes widening when she saw the crimson staining her sweater.

Kraven's jade stare narrowed towards what he immediately recognized to be blood smears and he seemed to wither before his expression turned fierce. He shook Darby once faintly and then again more intensely. He tried, but could scarcely speak her name.

It's-Kray…" Darby saw his fear. She was equally terrified but knew she had to get the words out. "It's not

A Lover's Hate

mine…it's not my blood," she looked down at the sweater again and stretched her hands out away from her body.

Seconds passed and then Contessa was screaming. The DeBurghs turned in time to see Fernando fall.

Kraven was alert at once, already noticing the color blooming black across the lower half of his friend's fleece hoody. County was on her knees, tugging at Fernando's clothes.

Kraven's attention was on getting the women to safety. Not an easy feat with Contessa refusing to let go of her husband.

"Fernando? Fernando talk to me! Ramsey!"

"County? Let's go, Darlin'- let's get you out of here," Kraven worked to maintain a fraction of calm. It was a pitifully useless attempt.

Contessa struggled against Kraven's hands under her arms as he tried to move her from Fernando's prone body. "No! Get off me!"

"Honey, I've got to get you inside-"

"I'm not leaving him, dammit! Kraven, no!"

Kraven pulled County from the ground seamlessly and in unison with collecting his wife. He carried Contessa at his side while he jerked Darby close to his chest. He turned his back to shield the women as he rushed them into the café.

"Obtenir une ambulance!" Kraven called for help as he rushed past the doors. His rough voice commanded quick action among the café staff. He carted the women to a rear booth. As County was a limp, trembling mass, he directed his instructions toward Darby.

"You two stay here- stay inside; do you understand me, Lass?"

A Lover's Hate

Darby's eyes darted around the café. Her feet tapped the floor at a frantic pace. Kraven brought his hands down hard on her thighs to capture her attention.

"You stay here, understood?" He nodded to encourage the gesture from her and kissed her mouth when she obliged.

Kraven returned to the scene where a crowd had already formed. He could hear the distinct shrill of police cars in route. A pool of burgundy had formed beneath Fernando's body. Kraven snagged a few of the heavy table cloths to drape over his friend.

"We're gonna keep you warm, man. Just stay with me, alright?" Kraven said the words for his benefit more than Fernando's. Remaining calm was essential.

"Stay with me, Fern." Kraven was tucking in the first of the cloths when he saw it. It hadn't been there before.

Slowly, he withdrew a small square piece of paper from just inside the hood of Fernando's pullover. Realization blossomed in Kraven's eyes as he scanned the words on the note.

For your attention, E.

Dear Reader,

Thank you for venturing a little farther down the rabbit hole that is the Ramsey/Tesano saga. Smoak and Sabra were so much fun to write. Blending these personalities was as exciting as it was amusing. It was a treat to craft their dialogue and a pleasure to craft their steamy sex scenes.

Sabra was already established as a mouthy, opinionated, alpha female. Pairing her with the likes of Smoak Tesano was definitely a challenge. Smoak has remained pretty much a mystery until now. Bringing him to life within the pages of this story was a thoroughly enjoyable experience. Of course he's beyond gorgeous but bringing to life his personality and demeanor was the real draw for me in writing him. I knew he'd have to be physically and intellectually arresting to tangle with Sabra.

The relationship was complex to say the least. The details of Smoak's and Sabra's history- as a couple and as children- were painful, dark and will be integral to the unfolding of the Ramsey Tesano plot. You're probably wondering about the ominous notes that have cropped up throughout the story. Who's behind them will be as unexpected as the details fueling the motive. Naturally, you have lots of questions about what this means for our beloved Fernando. Your answers are coming.

Love and Blessings,

AlTonya

altonya@lovealtonya.com

www.lovealtonya.com

ALTONYA'S TITLE LIST

Remember Love
Guarded Love
Finding Love Again
Love Scheme
Wild Ravens (Historical)
In The Midst of Passion
A Lover's Dream (Ramsey I)
A Lover's Pretense (Ramsey II)
Pride and Consequence
A Lover's Mask (Ramsey III)
A Lover's Regret (Ramsey IV)
A Lover's Worth (Ramsey V)
Soul's Desire (Ebook/Short Story)
Through It All (Ebook/Novella)
Rival's Desire
Hudson's Crossing
Passion's Furies (Historical)
A Lover's Beauty (Ramsey VI)
A Lover's Soul (Ramsey VII)
Lover's Allure (Ramsey Romance Novella)
A Ramsey Wedding (Novella)
Book of Scandal- The Ramsey Elders
Layers
Another Love
Expectation of Beauty (YA Romance)
Truth In Sensuality (Erotica)
Ruler of Perfection (Erotica)
Pleasure's Powerhouse (Erotica)
The Doctor's Private Visit
As Good As The First Time
A Lover's Shame (Ramsey/Tesano I)
Every Chance I Get
What the Heart Wants
Private Melody
Pleasure After Hours

FIND ALTONYA ON THE WEB

www.lovealtonya.com
www.facebook.com
www.shelfari.com/novelgurl
www.goodreads.com

An AlTonya Exclusive